D1034603

THE LONGEST DECEMBER

THE LONGEST DECEMBER

RICHARD CHIZMAR

CEMETERY DANCE PUBLICATIONS

Baltimore

❖ 2023 ❖

The Longest December
Copyright © 2023 by Richard Chizmar
Cemetery Dance Publications special edition

All rights reserved. No part of this book may be reproduced in any form or by any electronic or mechanical means, including information storage and retrieval systems, without permission in writing from the publisher, except by a reviewer who may quote brief passages in a review.

Cemetery Dance Publications
132B Industry Lane, Unit #7
Forest Hill, MD 21050
www.cemeterydance.com

The characters and events in this book are fictitious. Any similarity to real persons, living or dead, is coincidental and not intended by the author.

First Cemetery Dance Printing

ISBN: 978-1-58767-822-6

Cover Artwork and Design © 2023 by François Vaillancourt
Cover and Interior Design © 2023 by Desert Isle Design, LLC
Interior Artwork © 2023 by Mark Edward Geyer

Tuesday, December 3

I WOKE TO THE SOUND OF SLAMMING car doors outside and saw flashing lights reflected on my bedroom window and ceiling and thought one thing: Grant.

But Grant was at school in Richmond, two hundred miles away, and the logical part of my brain, which was obviously a lot more awake than the rest of me, told me to relax: if something had happened to Grant, they would have called to tell us, not shown up at the house in the middle of the night.

Besides, there were too many car doors and muffled voices now. Whatever was going on involved a lot more than just one vehicle.

I rolled over in bed and looked at the clock on the nightstand—11:53pm—then glanced at Katy, snoring quietly next to me. She was usually a light sleeper, and I was amazed she was still out. I guess a couple glasses of wine and three hours of late-night reruns of *The Office* will do that to you. Good for her.

I eased out of bed, feeling the cold shock of hardwood floor against my feet, and made my way over to the window. The December night had left a thin coating of frost on the outside of the glass, and I used my hand to wipe away condensation from the inside.

There were three police cars parked in my neighbor Jimmy's driveway, two of them with their bar-lights still flashing. As I watched, an unmarked sedan and a police van pulled up to the curb. Two people quickly exited the sedan and walked across the front yard, disappearing from my sightline.

I craned my neck for a better look, but I couldn't see whether they had gone inside the house or were merely gathered out on Jimmy's front porch. Wide awake now, I could feel my heart thumping in my chest. *What the hell was going on?*

As quietly as possible, I crept out of the bedroom and was halfway down the stairs when someone knocked on the front door. A single knock, not very loud.

I didn't even bother to look out the peephole. I unlocked the dead bolt and pulled open the door—

And found a smartly dressed woman standing on my front porch. She was tall and thin and had the reddest head of hair I had ever seen. She held up a badge and an identification card, and it took me a moment to realize she was talking.

"...Anderson. I'm sorry to bother you."

I pulled my focus away from the shiny police badge and blinked at her. "I'm sorry."

"Are you Robert Howard?"

The use of my name caught me off guard. "Yes...I am."

"My name is Detective Anderson, Mr. Howard. I'm sorry to bother you at this late hour, but it's important I talk to you."

I leaned forward and looked past the line of shrubs that lined my porch. Jimmy's front door was wide open, and officers were coming and going with focused intent.

"What happened? Is Jimmy okay?"

"Jimmy is your neighbor James Wilkinson, is that right?"

"Yes. Is he okay?"

Another police van glided to the curb, this time directly in front of my house. I noticed other house lights coming on up and down the street. Neighbors wearing robes and winter jackets starting to appear on front porches and gathering on the sidewalks.

"When was the last time you saw James Wilkinson, Mr. Howard?"

I had to think about it for a moment. "Let's see...he was here at the house all day Thursday for Thanksgiving, and then I saw him Friday evening when my wife and I got home from shopping. He said he was going to visit some friends for the weekend."

"And you haven't seen him since that Friday evening?"

"No."

"Heard from him? A phone call maybe?"

"No. Nothing."

"Did he mention where he was going or the names of the people he was planning to visit?"

I shivered in the cold air and shook my head. "No, he didn't. Can you tell me what's going—"

"We're serving a search warrant, Mr. Howard. Your neighbor, James Wilkinson, has been charged with two counts of murder. He is presently a fugitive on the run."

I couldn't help it—I laughed. "This has got to be some kind of mistake, detective."

"Unfortunately, not. I know this probably comes as a shock, but Mr. Wilkinson has been under surveillance for some time now. It was only through a combination of bad luck and incompetence that he evaded arrest this weekend. We've been watching his house for the past forty-eight hours in the hope he might return, but that hasn't been the case."

"This is crazy. Who did he supposedly murder?"

She ignored the question. "You have any idea where he might have gone, Mr. Howard?"

I pretended to think about it. "I have no idea. I still believe this has got to be a mistake. Jimmy's a good guy."

The detective reached into her jacket pocket and came out with a business card. Handed it to me. "We're going to need to ask you some additional questions, Mr. Howard. Tomorrow will be fine. Please call the office first thing in the morning. We'll set up a time." She turned away to leave.

"Wait a minute. Talk to me about what?"

She stopped and looked back at me. "It's my understanding that you're James Wilkinson's best friend, Mr. Howard. Is that correct?"

It suddenly made me nervous to admit the truth. "I guess so, maybe."

"That's why we need to talk to you, Mr. Howard."

She turned and walked away in the direction of Jimmy's house. I watched her go, then stared past her at the glow of the Henderson's red and green Christmas lights across the street. Their twinkling reflections blended with the flashing police lights, washing the frozen trees and lawns in festive, holiday colors. It felt like I was dreaming.

"Hey, what the hell's going on?"

I snapped out of my daze and looked over at Ken Ellis, my neighbor from down the street. He was wearing flannel pajamas and a robe. He stepped onto the porch next to me.

"Cold as a witch's titties out here. What that cop say to you? Something happen to Jimmy?"

I don't know why I lied, but I did. "She just said that she wanted to talk to me tomorrow. Didn't say what was going on."

Ken lifted his eyebrows. "*She*, huh? Chick cops are hot. She a looker?"

"Umm, I didn't really get a good look, Ken. She was in a hurry, I think."

"Well, I hope Jimmy's okay, buddy. I know you two are thick as thieves."

You're James Wilkinson's best friend, Mr. Howard...

Ken glanced back at the street. "Hey, there's Marcus. Fat bastard finally woke up." Already headed across the lawn, "I'll catch you later, Bobby."

I flipped a wave, walked inside and closed the door, relieved to be out of the cold and alone again.

I started up the stairs, then hesitated and walked to the front window. I pushed the curtains aside and watched as yet another cop car parked on the street. And I couldn't stop thinking: *this has to be some kind of mistake. It* has *to be.*

I was still thinking those same thoughts fifteen minutes later when four police officers walked out of Jimmy's front door carrying a pair of black body bags.

"THERE'S JUST no way," Katy said, her expression incredulous. "Jimmy can't even watch scary movies! You remember how he acted when we put on the *Poltergeist* remake Thanksgiving night?"

I nodded.

911
POLICE
911

"He was so spooked he made an excuse to leave early! No way. Jimmy couldn't hurt a fly."

"That's what I told the detective."

We were sitting across from each other on the bed. It reminded me of the early years of our marriage. Sitting in bed or on the sofa together, eating pizza and talking for hours and watching crummy late-night movies on cable television. It was about all we could afford back then, but it was enough. It was a pleasant thought to have on an otherwise shitty night.

I had awakened Katy a half-hour earlier when I finally came upstairs. Feeling numb, I told her everything the detective had said to me, but I left out what I had seen from the downstairs window. After all, it was dark outside; maybe my eyes had been playing tricks on me.

"You're sure she said two counts of murder?"

I nodded again. "I'm sure."

She looked down at her crossed legs, thinking, shook her head intently. "No, it's got to be a mistake."

"That's what I—"

"Oh my God, honey, you're going to have to call Grant in the morning. Tell him before it gets on the news. You know how much he loves Jimmy."

I *did* know. Jimmy was Grant's godfather. His friend. His mentor. "I'll call first thing."

Katy got up and went to the window. Peered outside for a moment. Turned around and said, "If Jimmy's a murderer, I'm Jack the Ripper."

I was too exhausted to laugh, but I managed a smile. "Come back to bed, you nut."

She listened and crawled in next to me. I covered us with a blanket, and we held onto each other in the dark.

"It's a mistake," she whispered, and a short time later she was snoring again.

She's right, I thought to myself. *It has to be.*

But then what was inside those body bags?

Sleep was a long time coming.

Wednesday, Dec 4

WE SAT at the breakfast bar and watched the morning news on television in stunned silence, our food going cold on the plates in front of us.

The story was everywhere. The announcers, with their oh-so-serious expressions and suitably grim tones of voice, had to work extra hard to keep their excitement in check. Every once in awhile, one of them would slip and you'd see the joy in their sparkling eyes or hear the glee in their giddy voices; they just couldn't help themselves.

The sound bites came at us one after the other:

James Wilkinson, age 60, a fugitive...

Charged with multiple counts of first-degree murder...

Body parts from multiple victims discovered in his basement workshop...

Authorities working to determine the victims' identities...

Multi-state manhunt under way...

Their words expertly interwoven with the stark images flashing on the screen:

A close-up of Jimmy's house in the early morning light.

A long panning shot showing a comfortable, middle-class neighborhood, including our own home.

Jimmy's faculty headshot from the university website, a bold black headline centered above it:

LOCAL MAN POSSIBLE SERIAL KILLER?

"Jesus, so now he's a serial killer," Katy said, pushing her plate away in disgust and getting up from the bar stool.

I gave her a minute, and then I followed her into the den where I found her standing in front of the fireplace, staring at the framed photographs on the mantle.

I came up behind her and hugged her, resting my chin on her shoulder. She wrapped my arms in her own arms and squeezed. Neither of us said a word.

There were three photos on the mantle: the first of Katy and I on our wedding day, youthful and smiling and scared to death; the second of two young boys, my brother and me, both of us bare-chested and tan and trying to look tough; and the third of Jimmy and Grant and me, standing on a pier somewhere in the Chesapeake Bay, each of us grinning like fools and holding up a stringer full of rockfish.

"I feel numb," she finally said, breaking the silence.

"Me too."

She took my hand in hers and turned around to face me. "Do you still think it's all a mistake, Bobby?"

I couldn't read her expression. I didn't know what she wanted to hear, so I just told her the truth. "I don't know."

I USED the remote control to open the garage door and warily drove out into the circus that had sprung up overnight.

There were cops everywhere next door. Some still filing in and out of the house, while others searched the garage and the shed out back. Two officers were using what looked like metal detectors in the flower beds and on the back yard lawn. Another was busy doing something on the roof.

Jimmy's entire yard had been lined with yellow police tape, and two big tents had been erected in the side yard. More cops gathered in and around the tents doing God knows what. The usually quiet street out front was crammed with nosy neighbors and reporters and television cameras. More police officers stood in the road, doing their best to control the crowd and direct traffic.

I slowly drifted down the driveway, trying to attract as little attention as possible, but as soon as the reporters noticed the open garage and my car, they swarmed toward me in a hungry pack. Panicked, I sped up, trying to escape, but had to stomp on my brakes when I discovered a WBAL news van was blocking my exit. I started blowing my horn.

Cameras and microphones slammed against my car windows. Frantic, sweaty faces pressed against the glass and screamed my name, machine-gunning questions at me:

"Robert…!"

"Did you have any idea?!"

"Bob…!"
"Do you know where he's hiding?!"
"Robert…!"
"Did you know?!"
"Bob…!"
"You had to know something…!"
"Robert…!"
"C'mon, give us two minutes…"
"What did you tell the police…?!"
"C'mon, don't be an asshole, Robert…"
"You were his best friend, you had to know something…"

A pair of baby-faced troopers finally arrived and corralled the reporters out of the driveway and away from my car. An older man with long, greasy hair climbed into the WBAL van and moved it out of my way.

I nodded my thanks to the troopers, turned right out of the driveway—*"You were his best friend, you had to know something…"*—and headed for police headquarters.

(TRANSCRIPT 17943C)—THE FOLLOWING TRANSCRIPT CONTAINS THE COMPLETE, UNEDITED INTERVIEW WITH WITNESS ROBERT JOSEPH HOWARD CONDUCTED ON DECEMBER 4, 2016. INTERVIEW CONDUCTED BY DETECTIVE LINDSAY ANDERSON (A3343). CORRESPONDING VIDEO FILES LABELED AS FILE 104A AND FILE 104B.

DETECTIVE LINDSAY ANDERSON: State your name for the record please.

ROBERT HOWARD: Bob…Robert Howard.

DETECTIVE: Age?

ROBERT: 49.

DETECTIVE: Occupation?

ROBERT: Regional Sales Manager at Stark Industries.

DETECTIVE: Residence?

ROBERT: 1920 Hanson Road, Edgewood, Maryland.

DETECTIVE: Marital status?

ROBERT: I'm married…to Katy Holt Howard. I don't know if you wanted her name or not.

DETECTIVE: That's fine, Mr. Howard.

ROBERT: Sorry. I'm a little nervous.

DETECTIVE: I understand. I want to first thank you for coming in today under such unfortunate circumstances. We certainly appreciate your cooperation.

ROBERT: You're welcome.

DETECTIVE: Do you have any children, Mr. Howard?

ROBERT: A son. Grant. He's a sophomore at Richmond University.

DETECTIVE: You are currently acquainted with a Mr. James Lee Wilkinson?

ROBERT: Yes…I am.

DETECTIVE: And what is your relationship with Mr. Wilkinson?

ROBERT: We're friends. He lives next door to me. At 1922 Hanson Road.

DETECTIVE: How long have you resided on Hanson Road?

ROBERT: Let's see…we bought the house in '05…so it'll be 12 years this spring.

DETECTIVE: And when did Mr. Wilkinson move into the house next door?

ROBERT: Oh, boy…I don't remember exactly…my wife probably

does...I would say somewhere around eight years ago. I know Grant was in middle school at the time.

DETECTIVE: So, Mr. Wilkinson moved into the residence at 1922 Hanson Road somewhere around 2008?

ROBERT: That sounds about right.

DETECTIVE: And that was the first time you had ever met Mr. Wilkinson? There was no prior relationship?

ROBERT: That's right. My wife and I met him on the day he moved in.

DETECTIVE: What was your first impression of Mr. Wilkinson?

ROBERT: He seemed like a nice guy. Older and a little quiet at first. Maybe even a little shy, like he wasn't used to being around people a lot.

DETECTIVE: You say that he was older. Can you provide any other background information regarding Mr. Wilkinson?

ROBERT: I know he was eleven years older than me and a widower. It felt like we didn't have a lot in common at first...but that changed with time. Ummm, what else? He said he and his wife had never had any children; she wasn't able to. She had died a few years before he moved to town. A heart attack in her sleep. He grew up in a small mill town in upstate New York; I can't remember the name. Lived there until he joined the Army and then lived all over the place until he got out. He ended up going to college to get a teaching degree.

DETECTIVE: Any specific family background?

ROBERT: Nothing very specific. He told me both his parents were deceased; he didn't talk about them very much, didn't have pictures of them around the house or anything like that. And he'd lost a younger sister to cancer right before he went into the Army. Her name was Mary, and he took her death very hard, I know that. They had been close growing up.

DETECTIVE: You mentioned that at first you didn't have very much in common with Mr. Wilkinson...but this changed in time?

ROBERT: It did. We became close friends.

DETECTIVE: And what do you attribute this closeness to?

ROBERT: Well, a lot of things, I guess. Proximity. You see a guy every day, even if it's just a wave hello, or the occasional beer shared across the fence, you get to be friends. And the more we talked, the more I think we realized we had a whole lot in common after all. We both liked fishing and golf. Photography. I taught him how to kayak; he taught me how to fly fish and play chess. We both liked history and documentaries. The first time he told me he was going to be teaching history part-time at the university, I threatened to enroll in all his classes. He laughed about that. Let's see, what else? We both came from broken homes, and we had both lost a sibling when we were younger. It was… something we didn't talk about a lot, but it was *there* between us…like an unspoken bond, I guess you could say.

DETECTIVE: I'm sorry, Mr. Howard. Did you also lose a sister?

ROBERT: No. (pause) My older brother drowned when I was ten years old.

DETECTIVE: Again, I'm very sorry. (shuffling papers) Okay, you say you both liked to fish and play golf and had an interest in photography. Did the two of you participate in these activities together? If so, how often and where?

ROBERT: Mostly, we just went fishing together. Usually over by the dam or we'd rent a boat and go out on Loch Raven Reservoir. Grant used to come with us a lot before he went away to school. He liked Jimmy quite a bit, and the feeling was mutual.

DETECTIVE: I understand that Mr. Wilkinson is your son's godfather.

ROBERT: Who told you that?

DETECTIVE: Some of your neighbors, I believe.

ROBERT: He is…but not in the traditional sense. Grant was never christened in a church or anything like that…but yeah we all agreed a couple years ago that Jimmy was Grant's de facto godfather. It's almost like an inside family joke.

DETECTIVE: So, you all went fishing together. How often did this occur?

ROBERT: Maybe three or four times a month during the summer. Less in the spring and fall.

DETECTIVE: No secret, secluded fishing spots for you and Mr. Wilkinson? A cabin tucked away in the woods somewhere?

ROBERT: No, nothing like that.

DETECTIVE: Okay, you mentioned golf and photography next.

ROBERT: Golf maybe once a month from spring to fall. He joked that we were better at watching golf on television and talking golf than we were at actually playing it. And photography was just something we talked about and traded books about. He was a lot more experienced than I was. He had a little darkroom in his basement and played around with developing his own photos. That's about it.

DETECTIVE: Did Mr. Wilkinson have any other friends? Any romantic ties? A dating life?

ROBERT: He played a lot of chess online, and poker with a regular group from the college. The game rotated from house to house, and I usually joined in when it was Jimmy's turn to host. But those were the only guys I ever saw over there. He liked his privacy, I know that. And women? No, I never saw any women at his house, nor did he ever really talk about women with me.

DETECTIVE: Why do you say Mr. Wilkinson liked his privacy?

ROBERT: He just seemed very set in his ways. Never unfriendly or anti-social, I don't mean that. My wife would tell you those words describe me a whole lot more accurately than Jimmy. He just...had his routines. He cut his lawn on Saturday mornings. He went to the grocery store on Thursday nights. He visited the library every other

Friday. He liked to be home by a certain time in the evenings. In bed by a certain time. Lights out by a certain time. He guarded his reading and writing time very closely.

DETECTIVE: (shuffling papers) What kind of writing was Mr. Wilkinson working on? Did you ever read any of his work?

ROBERT: Actually, no, I never did. I think it was too personal to share. He said he was keeping a journal, about his life, his experiences and travels, and I know he worked on it every evening.

DETECTIVE: Did he write on a computer? Notebooks? An actual journal?

ROBERT: I couldn't tell you.

DETECTIVE: Okay, you said Mr. Wilkinson never discussed other women with you. Did you get the feeling this was because he still felt loyal to his deceased wife?

ROBERT: I honestly couldn't tell you. Katy asked me the same question one day. All I know is that he rarely talked about his wife, and he never talked about other women. At least, not to me.

DETECTIVE: And Mr. Wilkinson never saw other friends except for the occasional poker game?

ROBERT: I know he played an occasional round of golf with friends from the college, but I got the feeling it was more of an obligation than a good time. And I believe he had some acquaintances from the library, but not like a regular book club or anything.

DETECTIVE: Did Mr. Wilkinson drink alcohol? Take drugs?

ROBERT: The strongest drug I ever saw Jimmy take was Nyquil and even then, he put up a fight. But you don't win many arguments with Katy, trust me. Drinking…in all the time I've known him, I probably saw Jimmy drink a total of fifteen, twenty beers. Never any hard liquor. And remember, that's over a period of maybe eight years. Jimmy took good care of himself; he was in great shape for a sixty-year-old.

DETECTIVE: Would you say Mr. Wilkinson was a religious man?

ROBERT: Not so much religious…I would say he was…spiritual. He was a pretty deep thinker. He could come up with some pretty heavy thoughts. He claimed to be a reformed Catholic. Had a big crucifix hanging in his den over the television.

DETECTIVE: Did he travel much?

ROBERT: Rarely. Maybe once or twice a year, he would visit an old Army buddy for the weekend or go on a solo fishing trip up north. He was excited last week at Thanksgiving, talked about going to see a couple guys from the old days.

DETECTIVE: Those were his exact words? A couple guys from the old days?

ROBERT: I think so, yeah. (pause) Maybe it was a couple Army guys from the old days. Or a couple guys from the old Army days. I'm not a hundred percent sure.

DETECTIVE: I want you to think very carefully about this next question, Mr. Howard. In all the years you lived next door to James Wilkinson, did you ever witness anything suspicious or alarming or disturbing?

ROBERT: (pause) No. Nothing.

DETECTIVE: Mood swings? Unusual displays of temper? Sneaking around?

ROBERT: Nothing.

DETECTIVE: Ever notice Mr. Wilkinson attempting to change his appearance in any way?

ROBERT: Never.

DETECTIVE: One final question, Mr. Howard. If you had only three words to describe James Wilkinson to me, what would they be?

ROBERT: (pause) Kind. Practical. (pause) Smart.

DETECTIVE: (shuffling papers) Well, that's all I have for now. I want to thank you again. I'll want to speak to your wife at some point, but we can do that at your home. No need for her to make the trip downtown. And I may want to ask your son a handful of questions over the telephone, but that can certainly wait.

ROBERT: That's it? I can go now?

DETECTIVE: Yes, sir, you're free to go. Oh, it's my understanding you had a little run-in with the press this morning. I'd prefer if you didn't talk to any reporters about this interview.

ROBERT: I don't intend to.

DETECTIVE: Thank you. And be sure to let us know if any of them bother you or your wife.

ROBERT: I will. Thank you.

END OF TRANSCRIPT 17943C

AFTER I called Katy and told her about the interview, I stopped at the McDonalds drive-thru and shot my diet all to hell. Two quarter pounders with cheese, large fries, and a chocolate milkshake. *Comfort food*, I told myself, and drove to the creek to eat in peace.

Winter's Run was a winding stretch of muddy water that ranged in depth from a couple feet to maybe ten at its deepest point. It mostly held catfish and carp and sunnies, but if you were lucky and knew what you were doing—pretty much the same thing when it came to fishing—you could pull the occasional largemouth bass or yellow perch out of its belly.

I had fished the Run since I was a young boy myself, and once Grant was old enough and patient enough to hold a pole, it soon became our favorite spot. I credit nostalgia and proximity for that little favor; Winter's Run was only a few miles away from our house.

I steered onto a gravel road that paralleled the creek for some distance and followed it until it turned into rutted, frozen dirt. Once I reached an enormous dead tree that looked like it had been struck by lightning, its bark blackened and peeling, I pulled over onto the weeds and turned off the car.

I had come to this spot with Jimmy several times before, when we were both in the mood to cast a line but didn't feel like driving far. I remembered that we had used corn and cheese balls for bait, hoping for a fat cat or carp to come along. Mostly, we had just talked and laughed and enjoyed the breeze and each other's company.

I sat there and ate my lunch and, despite the ninety-minute interview I had just completed, it felt like this was the first chance I'd had to take a deep breath and *really* think about my friend and the things he had been accused of.

Jimmy a murderer? A serial killer?! How was that even possible? This was a man I considered a part of my own family; a man I had seen almost every day for the past eight years. Wouldn't I have known…*something*?

I finished eating and made a mental note to throw away the trash before I got home, so Katy wouldn't see it. The last thing I needed right now was another lecture about my cholesterol. I took one final look at the slow-moving water and started the car. As I backed up onto the dirt road and pulled away, I realized that I'd forgotten to mention this particular fishing spot to the detective.

"THE DETECTIVE said they could either come tonight or tomorrow night. I said tomorrow."

"They?"

Katy was in the kitchen, making a salad at the big granite island she liked so much. The entire house smelled of her homemade tomato sauce.

"Her and her partner, she said. I felt like I was in an episode of CSI or something."

"That's what this morning at the station felt like. Like I was in a bad movie."

Sensing my exhaustion, Katy came over and hugged me, resting her head against my chest. "You should've heard Grant when I talked to him this morning. He was so upset. He said he's going to call you tomorrow."

"I keep thinking about some of the questions she asked. Did Jimmy travel a lot? Did I ever see anything suspicious? Did I ever see him sneaking around?"

"You poor baby." She gave me a good squeeze and returned to her salad. "I'm not looking forward to tomorrow night."

"It'll be okay, I'll be with you." She smiled and quickly looked away, and I could tell there was something else on her mind. "What are you thinking?"

Her hands started working faster, and I realized she was nervous. "Honey?"

She stopped and looked at me. "It's nothing, really."

"Tell me."

Deep breath. "I know how you feel about Jimmy...how we *all* feel about him."

"But?"

"No buts, nothing like that. It's just...when you said that, about the questions the detective asked you..."

"Which one?"

She glanced down at her hands for a moment, then met my eyes. "If you had ever seen him sneaking around."

I pushed off the counter where I was leaning and walked closer. "Did you?"

"Just...once."

"Jesus, honey, what did you see?"

"It's probably nothing." She shrugged, but I could see the tension in her face. "I was raking leaves in the back yard and the rake broke."

"I remember. Last fall"

"Well, I went next door to ask Jimmy if I could borrow his to finish the job, and his garage door was open. I guess I was kind of quiet about it because he didn't hear me walking up behind him. He was down on his knees, stretching to reach something underneath his work bench. I coughed to get his attention, and when he turned and saw me..."

"Yeah?"

"It was...just the look on his face, Bobby. He looked so angry and...*mean*. It was like he was someone else for a second or two, and then just like that it was gone, and he was Jimmy again."

"That's all?"

"Yeah, I told you it was probably nothing...but it was weird. It *felt* weird."

It was my turn to shrug my shoulders. "Could've been any number of things. A shitty day, or probably you just scared him."

She started to answer, and the phone rang. She grabbed the cordless from the counter behind her. "Hello? Hello?" She clicked it off. "No one there."

The conversation broken, she went back to finishing the salad, and I went back to salivating over her homemade pasta and sauce.

THREE HOURS later, fat and sleepy, I laid in bed waiting for the eleven o'clock news to come on and pretended I could understand what Katy was saying as she tried to talk and brush her teeth at the same time.

"Yes, dear. You're right, honey."

She rinsed her mouth and spit into the sink. "Oh, hush it. You don't even know what I just said."

I smiled. It was a nightly game we played, and it felt like a nice, warm, safety blanket after all that had recently happened in our world.

Katy turned off the light in the bathroom and settled into the bed next to me, taking her book from the nightstand. She had just enough time to finish a couple pages before the news came on.

Jimmy, of course, was the lead story.

As the Channel 11 anchor, a skinny, blonde with the unlikely name of Jessica Jones, did her best to sound intelligent, a photograph flashed on the screen behind her. It was a photo I had never seen before, most likely from a college faculty picnic: Jimmy, dressed casually in shorts and a t-shirt, captured in mid-throw, a Frisbee in his right hand. His arms looked lean and muscular, his face tan and intense, and I knew that was why the station had selected the picture.

Jessica Jones smoothly threw coverage to her reporter on the street, and a tall, black man with a microphone in his hand took over. I resisted the urge to look out the window and watch it live.

"Police, today, are reporting that evidence found inside James Wilkinson's house now indicate that there are at least three victims. That's right, three. Police officials refused to say whether this new discovery stemmed from human remains or additional forensic findings, but..."

"Jesus," I whispered, and Katy reached for my hand.

"Earlier this afternoon," the reporter continued, "I talked to one of James Wilkinson's colleagues at Washington College."

The screen flashed to a daytime shot with the college administration building framed in the background. The reporter towered over a middle-aged, bald man dressed in a tan sport coat.

"I'm standing here with Professor Jeremiah Robbins, head of the Washington College history department. Professor, I guess this has all come as a huge shock to you and your department..."

The Professor shook his head to demonstrate the severity of his disapproval. "That would be an understatement, to say the least. We are shocked and outraged at these findings."

Reporter: "And before this, how was Mr. Wilkinson viewed by his fellow teachers and students?"

Robbins: "I think it's very important to remember that James Wilkinson was merely a part-time employee of this institution. He did not carry a full class load and was actually only here on campus three days each week..."

Katy sat up in bed. "Those bastards are scrambling to distance themselves in any way they can."

"It's going to get worse," I said.

Jessica Jones was back onscreen now: "After a quick commercial break, we will talk to one of James Wilkinson's neighbors about the latest findings..."

"Ugh, turn it off, Bobby. I bet you anything it's that bitch, Frannie Ellis. She must've called five times today. I don't know who's worse, her or her perv of a husband."

I grabbed the remote control—and the telephone rang.

"Speak of the devil," Katy sighed. "I bet she's calling to tell us"—mimicking a high-pitched, annoying voice—*"she's going to be on television."*

I laughed and muted the television. I picked up the phone. "Hello?"

No response.

"Hello?"

No one there.

"Last time. Hello?"

I hung up.

"Thank God for small blessings," Katy said.

And then Frannie Ellis's chubby face filled our television screen, eyes as big as quarters, mouth moving with superhuman speed, hair all done up for the occasion.

"Ugh," Katy groaned, and rolled over to go to sleep.

Thursday, Dec 5

THE NUMBER of reporters in front of the house was down by at least half, and I made it to work the next morning with little trouble.

For the first half of the day, I distracted myself with catch-up phone calls and purchase orders, and it worked just fine. Co-workers interrupted a few times to ask questions—*"Don't you live on Hanson Road, Bob? How well did you know the guy?"*—but they were easy enough to blow off.

Grant called during his lunch break, and I talked him out of coming home early. Finish your exams and then come home, I told him. We'll catch up then.

But, by lunchtime, I found myself glancing out the second-floor window at the park below, daydreaming about Jimmy. And, as the afternoon passed, I found myself surfing the internet in an attempt to answer the pressing questions I had bouncing around inside my head.

I clicked the mouse and studied their faces carefully.

Jeffrey Dahmer.

Click.

Ted Bundy.

Click.

Arthur Shawcross.

Click.

John Wayne Gacy.

Click.

Dozens of victims. Murdered. Tortured. Butchered. Sometimes even eaten.

And the killers all looked so normal.

I had expected them to look like Boogeymen, but they didn't.

I found none of the answers I was searching for, and when four o'clock rolled around, I couldn't sign offline and get out of there fast enough.

As I was pulling out of the parking lot, a news teaser came on the car radio, promising another update on the hour about "the James Wilkinson Murders"—"*more information about the victims and an alleged Wilkinson sighting in Charlottesville, Virginia"*—so I switched it off and drove in silence.

At a stoplight, I glanced in the rearview mirror and noticed a blue car behind me. I saw it again ten minutes later, on the interstate. I wondered if it was following me.

Christ, it's all getting to you, I thought. *Making you paranoid.*

I exited the interstate and drove the several miles home checking the rearview. I didn't see the blue car again.

"I UNDERSTAND that you're often at home during the day, Mrs. Howard. Have you ever noticed any strange or unusual comings or goings next door?"

The four of us were seated in the den. Katy and I side by side on the sofa. Detective Anderson and her partner, Detective Hynd, on matching chairs centered in front of the fireplace. Detective Hynd looked like he'd just walked off a television cop show: tall, stocky, crew cut, with a first-class poker face. Just being in the same room with the guy made me nervous.

Katy had poured a cup of coffee for each of us. I had gone through mine in the first five minutes. Katy sipped at hers as she answered their questions. Neither detective had touched theirs.

Katy shook her head. "No, I really haven't. Jimmy was a creature of habit. I used to tease him about it all the time. I knew the days he worked at the college, and when he left the house on other days, I usually noticed his return within a couple hours."

"He never said anything inappropriate to you," Detective Anderson asked. "Even joking?"

"Never. Not once."

Detective Hynd this time: "Did he ever have any visitors that perhaps your husband didn't know about because he was at work?"

"Not that I noticed, no. I mean, it's possible, I guess. But pretty unlikely."

"I asked your husband to take his time and really think about this next question, and I'm asking the same of you, Mrs. Howard. In all the time that James Wilkinson was your next-door neighbor, did you ever witness anything at all out of the ordinary, anything unsettling or suspicious?"

Katy glanced away from the detectives, toward the large bay window that looked out over our front yard, body language I recognized as "leave me alone for a second, let me think."

When Katy finally looked back at Detective Anderson, she surprised me with her answer. "No. I can't think of anything. I'm sorry."

I felt her leg press against mine with the slightest of pressure.

"Well, that's all we really have," Detective Anderson said, getting to her feet. Detective Hynd followed suit, and I could feel him towering over me, even after Katy and I both stood up from the sofa.

"We appreciate your help, especially at this hour and in your home." Detective Anderson switched off her mini tape recorder and stuffed it into her jacket pocket.

"You're very welcome," Katy said, and walked the two detectives to the front door.

I KEPT waiting for Katy to tell me why she hadn't told the police about what she'd seen in Jimmy's garage, but I'd waited too long, and now she was sound asleep beside me.

I watched her snore for a while, then rolled over on my side, trying to get comfortable. Sleep felt a long way off for me.

My brain wouldn't stop thinking. Why hadn't she said anything to the detectives? On one hand, I was glad she hadn't told her story. It was probably nothing worth giving attention to. On the other hand, it bothered me—

—because I had remembered something, too. A moment in time that I'd completely forgotten, a moment that perhaps never even registered in the first place…until I listened to Katy's story about Jimmy in his garage…and then it all came back to me tonight.

Jimmy and I had been sitting in the center field bleachers at Camden Yards watching the Orioles play the Red Sox. It had been a cloudless Sunday afternoon, and the O's had been up by three runs in the top of the eighth inning. Six more outs and it went in the Win column.

The only blemish on an otherwise perfect day had been the pair of redneck drunks sitting behind us. We had tolerated their loud, slurred voices and cursing; we had put up with their catcalls and x-rated harassment of the Red Sox centerfielder; and we'd even turned the other cheek to a spilled beer that had soaked the game program I'd carelessly left on the ground at my feet.

But when one of them had spilled a full beer down the back of Jimmy's shirt and reacted with laughter and a high-five instead of an apology, we'd had enough. I'd shot to my feet and started to turn around, but before I could say a word, Jimmy was standing in front of me, his face a mask of barely contained rage, the drunk's neck grasped in Jimmy's right hand.

Before anything else could happen, two ushers were there to break it up and escort the drunks out of their seats. I remembered that the Orioles ended up blowing the lead, but won it in extra innings, and Jimmy and I had stopped at Chilis on the way home and stuffed ourselves sick with wings and barbeque ribs.

It's funny the things you remember—and forget.

Friday, Dec 6

THE SKY was an ocean of slate gray clouds, and it was starting to flurry as I drove out of my garage the next morning.

I stopped at the bottom of the driveway and took the newspaper from the paper box. It was safe to do now; most of the press was gone at this early hour. The television crews would be back later this evening to report live from in front of Jimmy's house, but when the around-the-clock police presence diminished so did the news vultures, as Katy now referred to them.

I glanced at the newspaper on the way in and wished I hadn't. Most of the front page was taken up by "the James Wilkinson murders." The boldest headline read:

KILLER STILL AT LARGE:
POLICE PREDICT MORE VICTIMS

I tossed the paper in the back seat. At least I had a busy day of work ahead of me. More than anything, I needed to redirect my brain away from images of Jimmy hiding something in his garage or losing his shit at an Orioles game. Both of which most likely meant absolutely nothing.

I pulled into the office lot twenty minutes early and parked in my usual spot. Only a handful of other vehicles had arrived ahead of me. I grabbed my briefcase and got out of the car—and nearly slipped on my ass.

A thin coating of snow had already accumulated on the grassy surfaces and was just now beginning to stick to the pavement. I looked around to see if anyone had witnessed my acrobatics, but I was alone in the parking lot. It was a peaceful sight with the falling snow and the hush of early morning stillness.

Already thinking about my morning conference calls, I grabbed my briefcase from where I had dropped it and started to walk toward the entrance doors—

—when a hand grabbed my shoulder from behind.

"Bob."

I nearly screamed and did a cartwheel, my feet pinwheeling beneath me. Spinning around, I held out my briefcase protectively in front of me.

"Hey, hey, I'm sorry. I didn't mean to spook you."

It was a man I had never seen before. My height. Curly hair. Glasses. Wearing an old Army jacket and holding a tape recorder.

"My name is John Cavanaugh. From the *Baltimore Sun*. I have some—"

"No," I said, unable to say more, trying to breathe again.

"It'll only take a minute, I promise."

I shook my head and started walking away.

"According to neighbors, you were Wilkinson's closest friend," he said from behind me, hurrying to catch up. "I just want to know what he was like. The person inside the monster."

I stopped and turned on him. *"The person inside the monster?* Jesus. Leave me alone."

I started walking again, faster now.

"Are you cooperating with the police, Mr. Howard? I understand they brought you in for questioning."

Questioning?

I kept walking.

"Your neighbors said you two were as thick as thieves. Is that true?"

I reached the entrance to my building and walked inside, praying he wouldn't follow. He didn't, but just as the front door was swinging shut, I heard his final question: "Why are you protecting him?"

ONCE I got over the shock and anger (and maybe a little embarrassment) of my run-in with the reporter—a thirty-minute phone call with Katy helped a lot—the day turned out pretty damn good.

Two of my morning phone conferences went off without a hitch, and the third, which I was dreading, ended up being postponed. I talked to Grant on the phone while I ate lunch at my desk and spent the afternoon reviewing purchase orders and a sales presentation that wasn't due until mid-January.

By the time I said goodbye to Janie at the front desk and walked outside, the skies had cleared, and the parking lot had been plowed. Maybe two inches of new snow blanketed the grassy areas.

I didn't think the reporter would still be waiting, but I wasn't taking any chances. I searched everywhere as I walked to my car, and I'll be damned if paranoia wasn't working its wicked charm on me again, because it felt very much like someone was watching me.

I hurried into the driver's seat, locked the door, and started the car. I didn't wait for the engine to warm up. I drove quickly out of the parking lot, that nagging feeling of being watched still itching at the back of my neck.

DINNER WAS a nice surprise—tacos and Katy's special margaritas. We ate at the coffee table in the den and watched the remake of *The Road Warrior* on pay-per-view. It was just what I needed, and I had Katy to thank for that.

As the end credits rolled on the television, I untangled myself from the blanket we were cuddling under and started clearing the dishes from the coffee table.

Katy sat up and yawned. "Just leave it, honey. I'll get it in the morning."

"I'm just gonna dump it all in the sink. It'll still be there in the morning."

She laughed. "Gee, thanks."

"Any time, babe." I gave her a wink and carried the dishes into the kitchen. I scraped the plates and bowls into the trash and left them in the sink.

"There is *something* you can do tonight, honey, if you're up to it."

I smiled and puffed out my chest. "And what might that be?"

She got up from the sofa and dramatically swung her hips as she walked upstairs. Over her shoulder: "You can take the trash out so the whole damn house doesn't stink in the morning."

I slumped. "Oh."

"HA, HA. You can take the trash out. *Real* funny."

I opened the lid on the garbage can sitting next to the garage and dropped in the zip-tied plastic bag. I replaced the lid and shivered in the frigid night air. The weather folks were calling for lower temps and more snow in the coming days.

Headlights flashed on the street below, and I watched as Ken Ellis's Escalade slowed and turned into his driveway across the street. He got out and hit the auto-lock on his remote and it chirped twice. He looked over at me and I gave him a wave. He stared for a moment, and then walked into his house without acknowledging me.

"Okay, that was weird," I mumbled to myself.

And then I heard something.

I stopped and listened—and heard it again.

A rustling in the bushes that bordered the front porch.

I glanced at the door to my house, light spilling out onto the porch, and moved to put myself between the door and the noise I had heard.

As I came around the side of the porch, I heard the sound again, and this time I could see the bushes shake ever so slightly. There was no breeze.

I walked closer, stooping down, preparing for fight or flight, but mostly wishing I had my cell phone on me.

I stopped and held my ground, listening.

Nothing.

I took another step—

—and was flung back on my ass on the snowy ground—

—as Mrs. Watkin's orange tabby sprung from underneath the bushes with a hiss and scampered past me, disappearing into the shadows.

"Fuck me," I hissed back at the cat, quickly pushing myself to my feet, embarrassed and pissed for the second time that day.

I brushed snow off my pants and looked around—thinking Katy's going to love hearing about this one—and my eyes settled on the dark, ground-level window at the side of Jimmy's house.

With little understanding of why I was doing it, I walked over to the window and peered inside. It was too dark in the house to see much, but I could make out enough details to see that the living room was a mess. Furniture moved. Drawers and shelves emptied. Papers and books and knick-knacks strewn all over the carpet.

I flashed back to the many times we had played poker in that same room…

Jimmy's buddies from the college complaining about the fatty snacks Jimmy had provided and that they'd had to bring their own beer. Jimmy joking that, despite all their degrees and teaching experience, I was the smartest guy in the room. All of us talking and laughing and farting—being guys and enjoying each other's company.

I stood there for a long time, remembering, until I couldn't feel my feet anymore. Then I went inside and got warm.

Saturday, Dec 7

WE SPENT the majority of Saturday out of the house. Out of town, as a matter of fact.

It was Katy's idea to drive up to Middlebury for lunch and some Christmas shopping. She scolded me for ordering onion rings and soda at the restaurant, and I told her we were even an hour later when she bought herself two new pairs of dress shoes. How many shoes does one woman possibly need? It's one of life's great mysteries.

All in all, it had been a near perfect day, and Jimmy's name hadn't come up once.

We got home long after dark, just in time for the early evening news and a tray of cheese and crackers in the den. Katy joked that we were celebrating; it was the first night in a week that there hadn't been any reporters camped out in front of Jimmy's house for a live broadcast.

When the news came on at ten o'clock, we were surprised for the second time that evening; Jimmy wasn't the lead story.

There had been a shooting at a New Jersey playground earlier in the day. Two adults and three children had been killed. Four others wounded. When it was over, the gunman had turned his weapon on himself. It was awful, and while I couldn't help but wonder why anyone would be outside at a playground in the middle of December, I didn't say anything. People were dead, kids for Godssake, and my heart ached for their loss.

Our run of good fortune ended after the commercial break—Jimmy was the second story. There had been another possible sighting, this time in southern Pennsylvania, coincidentally not far from where Katy and I had just spent most of our day.

Police officials were also planning a news conference sometime next week.

Then, a brief interview with another concerned neighbor, an elderly Korean gentleman who lived at the end of our block and who rarely ever spoke to any of us. But he sure had plenty to say to the camera, very little of which was probably the truth.

They saved the biggest surprise for last...

Because there I was in full techno-color, a terrified expression on my face as I sat inside my car blowing the horn at the frenzy of reporters blocking the driveway.

I almost choked on my cheese and crackers.

Katy put a hand to her mouth. "Oh my God."

I sat there in shock as a close-up of my face filled the screen, and a television audience listened to me yelling, "No comment!" in a pathetically shaky voice.

"According to several sources," the news anchor explained, "Robert Howard is not only James Wilkinson's closest neighbor, but also his closest *friend*. Up until this point, Howard has declined to comment, but sources report that Howard *is* cooperating with authorities and will be..."

Katy clicked off the television. "Fucking vultures. I told you." She turned to me. "Are you okay?"

I nodded. "I'm fine...just a little surprised is all."

"I guess until the cops have that news conference, they're scrambling to come up with any story angle they can find."

"I guess so." I got up from the sofa, legs shaky, and started turning off the lights.

Katy carried the tray and plates into the kitchen. "Uh, oh, your staff is going to be buzzing at work tomorrow."

I groaned. "I hadn't even thought of that." I switched off a floor lamp by the den window—

—and froze.

A shadow was moving in the bushes outside—and it was a lot bigger than a cat this time.

"Just tell them you didn't want to get into it with them and—"

I dropped to a knee in front of the window and "*sshhed*" Katy.

She looked confused. "What is it?"

"I think there's someone outside," I whispered.

She started walking toward me.

"No, no, stop right there."

I peered over the windowsill—and there it was again. A dark shadow creeping closer now. Definitely a person.

"Call 911. Tell them to hurry."

She rushed back into the kitchen, and I could hear her voice cracking as she talked to the emergency operator. She hung up, and said, "Three minutes."

"I'm sure it is but go double-check the front door's locked." I listened to her footsteps grow fainter, and then I snuck another peek over the windowsill—

—and found myself face to face with the curly-haired reporter from the parking lot. He looked as surprised as I did.

This time, I screamed. I couldn't help it.

So did Katy.

And then the front yard was flooded with flashing lights and loud voices and swarming with cops, and the reporter was turning around and holding his hands up in the air.

"AND YOU'RE sure you don't want to press charges, Mr. Howard?" The officer stopped scribbling in his notepad long enough to give me a questioning look. I glanced at Katy, and she shrugged her shoulders. We were both exhausted.

The three of us were standing in the foyer, the front door closed to the chaotic scene outside.

The reporter, John Cavanaugh, was handcuffed in the back seat of a patrol car parked at the curb. Up and down the street, neighbors stood in clusters, drawn by the flashing lights and the hope of more drama. And, of course, the vultures were back, television cameras rolling, microphones humming, hairspray clogging the chill night air. It was a circus atmosphere all over again.

"I don't think so. I just want to be done with it."

The officer flipped his notebook closed. "Okay, but if you change your mind, call us in the morning." He opened the door and grinned at us. "I think we'll hang onto him overnight, let him sweat a little bit."

I smiled back at him. I liked that idea a lot.

Monday, Dec 9

SUNDAY PASSED in a blur of football games and naps and ignored phone calls and emails. I never set foot outside the house the entire day, and the only time Katy left was to deliver sandwiches and drinks to the two police officers camped out in their patrol car at the bottom of our driveway. By late evening, with the temperature plummeting to single digits, most of the press had gotten the hint and cleared out. We'd managed to avoid the news all day and were in bed by eight o'clock, asleep before nine.

So, when the alarm clock buzzed on Monday morning at 6:30, we'd hit the ground running, feeling rejuvenated and hopeful.

After a busy morning of cleaning house and paying bills, Katy was spending the afternoon at a friend's house, playing Hearts and binge-watching *Game of Thrones*.

All morning at the office, I had faced a barrage of questions from my co-workers—*"Why didn't you tell us? What was he like? Did you have any idea? Do you think he's still alive? Are you sure you're telling us everything?"*—but eventually the questions had run dry, and the work-day had returned to some semblance of normality.

I was able to eat lunch in peace, and now I sat at my desk, adjusting fourth quarter purchase orders and answering nosy emails I had ignored yesterday.

There was a knock at my office door. I looked up and saw Janie coming in with a file I had requested earlier this morning. "This what you needed, boss?"

I glanced at the name on the file. "Bingo. Thanks for tracking it down."

"Tis my job." She remained standing in front of my desk, and I knew she had more to say.

"Something on your mind, Janie?"

She shook her head. "I just couldn't believe when I saw the news yesterday. I couldn't believe it was you they were talking about."

"Yeah," I said, fidgeting. "It's been an interesting week to say the least."

"Well, listen, if you ever need someone to talk to...I've read a lot of true crime books, like dozens of them, plus I belong to some online groups, so if you ever need to share, I'm right here."

"I appreciate the offer, but I'm—"

My cell phone rang. I gestured at it apologetically and Janie whispered, "Talk later" and scurried out of the office.

My cell phone rang again, and I picked it up from the desk beside me. Looked at the caller ID: *Unknown Caller.*

"Hello?"

No response.

I suddenly remembered the hang-ups at the house from the week before.

"Hello?"

Nothing.

"Hel—"

Click.

I pushed the OFF button and stared at the phone.

"BOBBY! HOLD on a second!"

I was halfway across the parking lot when I heard someone call out my name. I stopped and turned around, bracing for the worst, but it was only Janie chasing after me in her high heels and mini-skirt. Her face was beet red, and she was breathing heavy.

"You forgot this in the break room," she said, skittering to an unsteady stop. She handed me a file folder labeled: ROTO-MAIL Account.

"What would I do without you?" I asked, taking it from her.

"Probably run around in circles most days." She started fixing her hair, which was a swirling mess in the cold December breeze.

"Get back inside before you freeze to death."

She hesitated, a strange look on her face, and I knew the forgotten file folder wasn't the only reason she'd followed me out to the parking lot.

"I also wanted to apologize."

"For what?" I asked.

"For before. In your office. I must've come off a little ghoulish in my eagerness to talk about your friend, but I swear I didn't mean it that way."

I waved her off. "It's fine, Janie. Everyone's curious and excited to talk about Jimmy. The problem is I have no idea what to say. I've been blindsided…by all of this."

"How's Katy handling it?"

"Not very good," I said, shaking my head.

"You'll call me if there's anything I can do to help either one of you."

"I promise."

I shooed her inside and drove home.

KATY TURNED off her light and rolled over to face me in the dark. Outside, a strong wind howled in the trees and buffeted the upstairs windows.

"Do you remember our first apartment?" Katy asked. "Up on the fourth floor."

"Of course, I do. Brittany Place, Greenbelt's finest apartment complex."

She laughed. "The wind tonight reminds of back then. Remember how it used to keep us awake at night. We were so young…scared to death and fearless all at the same time."

"Things haven't changed that much, have they?"

She thought about it for a moment. "I guess not."

"I think we're hanging in there pretty darn—"

The phone rang.

Katy groaned and reached for it on the nightstand.

"Hello?"

She waited.

"Hello?"

She hung up.

Neither of us spoke, and I knew she was thinking the exact same thing I was.

"Do you think it's him?" she finally asked in the darkness, and I found myself wishing I could see her face.

"Him? Jimmy?"

"Yeah. Sometimes it happens during the day, too, when you're at work."

"Probably just reporters, honey."

"Maybe. Can I ask you something?"

"Anything."

A long pause.

"Do you think he did it?"

I laid there, thinking.

"Bobby?"

"I don't know."

Thursday, Dec 12

THE GPS told me to turn right in 200 feet, so I listened and turned right, but I remained skeptical. The damn thing had had me driving in circles for the past half hour and now I was in danger of being late for lunch. A lunch I couldn't afford to be late for. I was scheduled to meet with the vice president of Canton Industries, a joining of the minds that had taken nearly two months to arrange. The proposal I had put together was maybe the best work I had ever done; now I just had to get my ass to the restaurant and close the deal.

The past couple days had been relatively peaceful, which was a godsend after what had happened Saturday night. Katy was finally starting to feel relaxed in the house again. The press had quieted down, and there had been no more phone calls or late-night visitors. I had actually slept soundly last night and was feeling energized for my meeting.

The GPS told me to turn left in eight-tenths of a mile. I told it to "kiss my ass" and changed lanes—and that's when I noticed the blue car in my rearview mirror.

Instinctively, I slowed down—and the blue car slowed down behind me. Keeping pace. I studied the mirror, trying to determine if it was the same blue car I'd seen the week before.

"Your destination is located one-tenth of a mile on the right."

I looked up and, sure enough, there was the restaurant. "I'll be damned." I checked my watch: four minutes to spare.

"You have reached your destination."

I switched on my turn signal, glanced in the rearview mirror—and the blue car was gone. A silver minivan had taken its place.

I swung into the Giovanni's parking lot and hurried inside exactly one minute early.

TWO-AND-A-HALF HOURS later, I was kicked back in my office chair with my feet up on the desk, feeling like the king of the world.

The meeting had gone well.

The meeting had gone *very* well.

Charlie Kennedy, Canton Industries VP, had shook my hand in the Giovanni's parking lot after lunch and promised a sizeable order no later than Monday afternoon. And if that wasn't blessing enough, he'd also called my boss at Corporate from his car and praised my sales proposal as one of the smartest he had ever seen.

Janie and several co-workers had greeted me like a conquering hero upon my return to the office. I couldn't wait to get home tonight and surprise Katy with the news.

I adjusted myself in the chair and closed my eyes, letting the warm feeling of success wash over me. It felt good to feel good about something again.

Before long, I felt myself dozing and didn't fight it.

THE BUZZING of my cell phone woke me a short time later. I dropped my feet to the ground and sat up, wiping sleep-slobber from my chin. I snatched up my phone and saw that I had received a text message.

I tapped the screen and read: I KILLED THEM.

My heart trip-hammered in my chest. I read it again to be sure, then typed: *Who is this?*

I KILLED THEM ALL.

My hands were shaking. *Who is this?*

YOU KNOW WHO THIS IS.

Jimmy?

YOU KNOW.

What do you want?

WHAT DO YOU THINK I WANT?

???

YES YOU DO.

Tell me what you want.

I WANT YOUR BLOOD.

My finger froze over the phone screen.

OR MAYBE…

What?

KATY'S BLOOD.

The sight of Katy's name broke the paralysis of fear that was gripping me and spurred me to action. I grabbed my briefcase and headed for the parking lot, ignoring Janie's concerned questions as I hurried out of the front office.

As I jogged toward my car, I tapped HOME on the cellphone screen and listened to it ring. Once. Twice. Three times. "C'mon, pick up." It rang two more times, and I hung up and called Katy's cell phone.

She answered after the first ring. "Hey, baby, I was just thinking about you—"

"Where are you?"

"What? What's wrong?"

"Where are you?!" I started the car and peeled rubber out of the parking lot.

"I stopped at the grocery store on the way home from Kelly's. I'm just now pulling into the neighborhood."

"Listen to me very carefully. The first thing I want you to do is look around and make sure no one is following you."

"Following me? What—"

"Do it, Katy!"

"Okay, okay!" A pause, and then: "There's no one behind me at all. And I can see all the way to both ends of Bayberry."

"You're sure. No blue cars? Nothing at all?"

"I'm sure, baby. Now tell me what is going on."

I hit the interstate and cranked my speed to ninety.

"I want you to stay on the line with me and stay inside your car when you get home. Don't pull into the garage. Park at the curb and wait for me there. I'll be home in ten minutes..."

DETECTIVE ANDERSON sat across from Katy and me at the kitchen table and listened to someone talking on the other end of her cell phone. After a moment, she said, "I want it faster," and hung up without saying goodbye.

She looked up at us, face grim, all business.

"We're working with the phone company to trace the texts. Most likely it was a burner phone, but there are ways to track down where the phone was purchased and activated. It's not foolproof, but it's what we got."

She pulled several sheets of paper from a file folder. "Sign these and we'll put a trace on your phone. He calls or texts again, we'll find him. We'll also be able to record anything he says to you."

I picked up a pen and signed the papers.

Friday, Dec 13

I HEARD Katy crying before I reached the bottom of the stairs. Panicked, I rushed into the kitchen and found her slumped against the dishwater, her face buried in her hands. Everything felt like a bad dream again.

I sat on the floor beside her and wrapped her in my arms. "It'll be okay, I promise."

She cried harder, trembling.

"That's it, let it out."

She looked up at me, her face smeared with tears and snot. She pointed a finger at the television on the kitchen counter. "It's all over the news. They even know what the texts said."

I opened my mouth to say something, but nothing came out.

"My mom called three times. She's worried sick."

"We'll go over there later today and talk to her. We'll make it okay."

"And Heather called and said everyone in the neighborhood is talking about us...saying things."

"What kind of things?" I asked.

She started crying again. "That...that we're playing up to the press, trying to get attention. First being all mysterious and then accusing a reporter of being a stalker and now the texts."

"That makes no Goddamn sense."

"I knowwww." Sobbing again. "She also said that Ken Ellis was telling people you were a suspect; that you and Jimmy were thick as thieves."

I remembered the curly-haired reporter using those exact same words. *Ken, you lousy, big mouth son-of-a-bitch.*

"I'm scared, Bobby."

I brushed my wife's hair out of her face and used my hand to wipe her cheeks, and then I sat there on the kitchen floor and rocked her in my arms until the tears stopped coming.

I CALLED out of work. Paced around the house. Checked on Katy to make sure she was resting. Looked out the bedroom window to make sure the patrol car assigned to guard our house was still parked at the curb. Talked to Detective Anderson on the telephone. She apologized for the leak to the press. She had no idea where it had come from, and I could tell she was as angry as we were.

After lunch, I went out to the garage and looked for something to do. I felt lost. I felt like my brain wasn't working the way it was supposed to.

I straightened the tools on my work bench (the work bench Jimmy had helped me build). I moved cases of bottled water from one spot on the floor to another spot on the floor. I hung a snow shovel on the wall hook where it belonged. I swept the floor.

I noticed a couple boxes of Grant's old school papers on the floor and cleared space on a shelf for them. I bent over to pick up the first box, and on my way back up, I nailed my head on the blade of the snow shovel.

"Goddammit!"

I flung the box away, papers scattering everywhere, and swiped an angry hand at the wall, sending the shovel clattering to the ground. I lunged forward and kicked the cardboard box, sending it flying against the opposite wall of the garage. I spun around to look for something else to hit—

—and Detective Anderson was standing at the top of the driveway, staring into the garage at me.

"Everything okay, Mr. Howard?"

I touched a sore spot on the back of my head, checked my fingers for blood. "I'm fine," I said, embarrassed. "Hit my head, lost my temper."

She looked like she wanted to say something else, then changed her mind. Instead, she held out a file folder and said, "Do you mind if we go inside? Few things we need to talk about."

I LEFT Detective Anderson sitting in the den and went upstairs to get Katy. Once again, we sat together on the sofa across from the detective and waited for her to tell us why she'd come.

"First thing, I have some good news. The texts were a prank."

Katy sat up straight beside me. "A prank?"

"That's right. College kid over at Morgan State. Wannebe film director. Making a slasher film for his senior project. Thought it would be 'cool' to try to scare you."

"It worked," Katy said.

"He paid for the phone with his parents' American Express card. Was easy enough to track. The kid's remorseful, and stupid. Up to you if you want to press charges."

I looked at Katy, but she didn't say anything. I could tell she was relieved. I just felt angry.

"I also came to show you these," the detective said, spreading four glossy photos across the coffee table.

The photos were of three young women and a man who looked in his late 20's. Based on the clothing and hairstyles, the pictures looked at least five or ten years old.

"Recognize any of these people? Ever seen any of them next door at the Wilkinson's?"

I studied the photos and shook my head. "Not me."

"Me either," Katy said.

"You're positive?"

We both nodded. "Yes."

Detective Anderson collected the photographs and returned them to the folder. Looked at me. "The *real* James Wilkinson hasn't tried to contact you, has he, Mr. Howard?"

"What? No." I could feel Katy staring at me.

"If he does, you would never try to help him, right?"

It felt like the temperature in the room had gone up at least ten degrees. I didn't trust my voice to answer, but I knew I had to. "Of course not."

"That's good to hear."

The detective got to her feet. I thanked her for bringing us good news for a change and walked her to the front door, anxious for her to leave. She walked out onto the porch, stopped and turned around. "By the way, what was your brother's name, Mr. Howard?"

"My brother?"

"The brother you lost when you were young. What was his name?"

"What does that have to do with anything?"

Her face remained blank. "Just doing my job, Mr. Howard."

I glanced back at Katy sitting on the sofa. She was watching us. "My brother's name was James."

Saturday, Dec 14

ADHERING TO the kind of unspoken agreement that only decades-long married couples can employ, Katy and I never discussed the people in the photographs, and the next time we saw their faces, we were in bed watching the news—and a fifth face had joined them. Another young woman, pretty, with glasses and a scattering of pale freckles across her nose and cheeks.

The headline above the faces read:

POLICE NOW IDENTITY FIVE VICTIMS

Francis Lund, Teresa Thompkins, and Susanne Worthy were from Pennsylvania, Karen Hunter was from Delaware, and Frank Hubbard was from western Maryland. They had been identified from DNA remains found at both Wilkinson's home and a storage unit he'd rented in nearby Fallston. The oldest victim, Lund, had been killed approximately nine years ago, and the most recent victim, Hunter, just over two years ago. An unnamed police source indicated that several additional victims could soon be identified.

The telephone on the nightstand rang, and we both ignored it. After four rings, it stopped.

Katy turned off the television, and we laid in silence for a long time. I listened to the rhythm of her breathing soften and thought she was asleep—but then she surprised me and spoke in a whisper, "Shouldn't we tell the police about the hang ups?"

I pretended to be asleep—and didn't answer.

Sunday, Dec 15

THE TEMPERATURE was in the mid-30's, and a sheen of ice glittered in the bird bath at the corner of the back yard, but the morning sun felt good on my face. I was supposed to be repairing one of Katy's rose trellises out by the shed, but I couldn't stop myself from thinking about the five faces I'd seen last night on television (something about those freckles had really stuck with me), and my eyes kept wandering past the fence to Jimmy's back yard.

Streamers of police tape fluttered in the breeze. His shed was wrapped in the bright yellow tape and padlocked. I had helped him build that shed several summers ago, and he had recently helped me pick out mine from Home Depot.

My cell phone rang inside my coat pocket. I considered letting it go, then thought better of it: *what if it was Katy calling from inside?*

I put down the hammer and took out my phone. Looked at the caller ID: *Unknown Caller.*

I hit the ACCEPT button, ready for another hang up.

"Hello?"

Nothing. Of course.

"Hello."

I started to hang up and heard: *"I'm sorry."*

Startled, I almost dropped the phone.

"What? What did you say?"

"I'm sorry, Bob. You have no idea how sorry I am."

This wasn't a prank: I knew Jimmy's voice.

"Then…why?"

"I couldn't help it. I wish I had a better answer, but I don't. I owe ***you*** *the truth at least."*

"You have to turn yourself in, Jimmy."

"Believe me, I've thought about it."

"All the calls and hang ups…it's been you?"

"I missed hearing your voices."

"I have to tell the police you called."

"Hell, they probably already know after that texting fiasco. I was sorry you had to go through that."

"Where are you?"

Jimmy laughed. *"Do you remember that day we went fishing out by the dam? Caught all those fat channel cats and you fell in trying to unsnag your line? And on the way home you almost ran over that baby deer and we ended up chasing it into the woods so it would be safe, laughing and yelling and acting like a couple of idiot kids?"*

"Yeah, I remember."

Deep breath. *"That was a really good day, Bobby. I almost felt okay that day."*

My heart felt like it was breaking. "We can get you help, Jimmy."

"Nah, there's no help for me, old friend. There never was. Nothing left now but penance."

"But if you turn yourself in, if you cooperate, maybe there's a chance—"

"My chances were all used up a long, long time ago, Bobby." Deep sigh. *"It's such a beautiful day outside. I'm glad you're spending it in the yard."*

"How did you know I was—"

The phone went dead in my hand.

I DIDN'T tell Katy about the phone call. I didn't want to worry her, and I guess if I was being honest with myself, I didn't tell her for other reasons, too; I just couldn't quite figure out what those other reasons were.

I made an excuse to leave the house for a short time and arranged to meet Detective Anderson at the diner down the street. She was waiting for me when I got there.

"And how can you be so sure it wasn't meant as a threat?"

"I just don't think it was," I said, sipping my coffee.

"He was obviously close by. Either watching you while you talked, or he'd seen you in the yard a short time earlier."

"Right." I shrugged. "And if he'd wanted to do something to me, he would have had ample opportunity."

Detective Anderson's face hardened. "I know this is still difficult for you to process, Mr. Howard, but this man is *not* your friend. He is *not* the man you believed him to be."

I didn't say anything.

"He is the subject of a multiple jurisdiction manhunt, and he risked capture to see and talk to you. That fact speaks very loudly to me."

"I don't know what to tell you," I said, trying not to sound defensive.

"I want you to look at something."

She slid a stack of glossy photographs across the table. I picked them up and flipped through them.

They were murder scene photos: numerous angles of a young girl laying naked on the ground, her face hidden beneath long, blonde hair, her body and the floor around her smeared with blood. She almost looked like a Barbie Doll. Like she wasn't real. The last photograph took care of that: a close-up of her face, probably a school picture, smiling and happy, looking very real, indeed.

"Lisa James. Seventeen-years-old. From Leesburg, Virginia. Straight 'A' student headed to Dartmouth in the fall. She was killed eight years ago in a utility shed outside the community pool she lifeguarded at."

I swallowed and slid the photographs back to her.

"Her case had been unsolved until yesterday, when forensic evidence linked James Wilkinson as her killer."

She gathered the photos and got up from the table.

"You remember that next time Wilkinson calls you…or you find yourself thinking of him as your old fishing buddy."

MONDAY, DEC 16

AN UNMARKED police car followed me to work in the morning, and then followed me home again just over an hour later, after a brief meeting with my boss.

"You hit it out of the park, Bob. Charlie Kennedy couldn't stop singing your praises, and trust me, that old bastard doesn't even like his own kids."

"Then why not let me work straight through Christmas Eve, like everyone else?"

"Everyone else isn't dealing with the mess you're dealing with. Besides, you deserve the time off after this sale."

I knew better than to argue with him. I was becoming a distraction. It was easier to give me an extended, paid vacation than deal with tapped telephone lines and undercover cops roaming around the building and parking lot. Not to mention my panicked exit from the office the other day. Janie said I'd nearly given her a heart attack running out the way I did.

"So, I'm not back until January 6?"

"That's right," he said, slapping me on the shoulder. "New year, new quarter, new time to kick some ass!"

Sometimes, I hated my boss.

THE HOUSE was too quiet. I couldn't stand it.

Katy was spending the day with her mother, and I didn't want to interrupt their time together just to whine about my job. I figured I could whine plenty to her tonight when she got home.

I tried to watch one of the afternoon soaps I always heard Janie raving about at the office but gave up by the second commercial break. I got up and poured myself a drink. Katy would've been shocked—hell, I was pretty surprised myself—but I thought I deserved a drink after the past couple weeks. Maybe I would even have two and take a nap.

I carried my glass back into the den and stopped in front of the fireplace. Took down one of the photos from the mantle. I could hear the ticking of the miniature grandfather clock behind me in the foyer.

"The brother you lost when you were young. What was his name?"

I heard the detective's voice in my head as I stared at the old photograph. My brother and me at the lake on a hot summer day. Bronzed by the sun. Crooked, trying-to-look-tough smiles. His arm around my shoulders. Wearing his favorite Baltimore Orioles floppy hat and his good luck lightning bolt pendant around his neck.

We looked like young gods. We looked like we would live forever.

Tuesday, Dec 17

BAGELS AND coffee at the breakfast bar—and admission time. I would've rather swallowed shards of broken glass.

"He called you?" Katy's voice shrill; the expression on her face incredulous. "When? What did he say?"

I started to answer, but she interrupted. "And why in the hell didn't you tell me?"

I put my hands up. "Calm—"

"Don't you dare tell me to calm down."

I slid off the stool and started pacing. Like a twelve-year-old boy in big trouble, which is exactly how I felt.

"I didn't tell you right away because I didn't want you to worry. I knew how stressed you were."

"When?"

"Sunday morning. When I was working out back on your trellis."

Shaking her head. "Oh my God."

"Honey, I didn't want you to worry. I even told Detective Anderson that I was—"

"You told the cops, but not me?" Her voice rising again.

I stopped pacing. "I had to…to be safe. They searched the neighborhood. Quietly, so no one would be alarmed. They even put up roadblocks in case he was still in town."

"Jesus, Bobby, what did he say to you?"

"He said he was sorry, he said—"

"He said he was *sorry*?" A mocking expression on her face I had never seen before.

"He said he was sorry and was thinking about turning himself in. You can listen to the entire phone call. Detective Anderson has the audio file."

"And you didn't tell me because you were worried?"

"That's right, baby. But I knew I couldn't keep it from you for long."

"Did you ever think that I'm worried about *you*, Bobby?"

"Worried about what?"

She looked away for a moment, then met my eyes again. "Your state of mind for starters."

"What are you talking about?"

"Why aren't you scared, Bobby? Why aren't you worried about yourself in this whole thing? I know you loved him like a brother. I know you looked up to him like a brother. But you saw the pictures. You heard the reports."

"If he was going to hurt us, Katy, he would've done it a long time ago."

"How do you know that? How do you *know*?"

"C'mon, he lived a hundred feet away from us for eight years."

"You don't know that, Bobby. You don't know *him*. None of us did. He's not who we believed he was. He's…a monster."

Thursday, Dec 19

GRANT DUMPED his duffle bag and knapsack in the foyer and hugged his mother. "Sorry I'm late. Again."

Katy laughed and squeezed him tighter. "That damn car of yours."

"Nothing wrong with that car a brand new engine won't fix."

I chimed in. "And a battery and a muffler and a—"

We all laughed, and it was music to my ears after the last couple days of strained conversation and uncomfortable silence in the house.

Grant kissed his mom on the cheek, and then it was my turn for a hug. I noticed that he held on a little tighter and longer than usual.

"Good to see you, Pop."

"You, too. You, too."

He gestured outside the window at the police cruiser parked at the curb. "What are they doing here?"

Katy glanced nervously out the window, while I gave him my best brush off. "Just routine. Tell you after dinner."

He tilted his head back. "Speaking of dinner, what is that amazing smell?"

Katy picked a fuzz ball off the shoulder of Grant's sweater. "Why don't we head into the kitchen, and you can see for yourself?"

"Don't have to ask me twice." And off he went.

Katy and I smiled and followed Grant out of the foyer. It felt good to be a family again.

THE DOOR to Grant's bedroom was ajar, but I knocked anyway.

There was no response at first, and for a moment I thought he might have fallen asleep early or perhaps he was using the bathroom down the hall. Just when I was about to knock again, I heard a rustling noise and a muffled voice: *"Come in."*

"Just checking to see if you need anything," I said, pushing open the door and stepping inside.

He was standing at the foot of the bed, sorting through a messy pile of clothes. His empty duffle sat off to the side next to a stack of spiral notebooks and the shaving kit I had given to him last Christmas. He'd taken off his shoes and I could see that he was wearing two different colored socks. One of them had a hole in it and his big toe was sticking out. "I'm all good, thanks."

"Mom told me to tell you that dessert is ready, and she left clean towels in the bathroom in case you want to shower."

He looked up at me and smiled. "I know where the towels are, Dad."

"Hey, I'm just the messenger," I said, putting my hands up in the air.

"Sometimes, I think Mom still thinks I'm away at summer camp instead of college."

I laughed. "Your mom is very aware that you've grown into a mature young adult. She just misses you." I stared at him for a moment and felt a tightening in my chest. "We both do."

"And I miss you guys back," he said, smiling and guiding me out of the bedroom. "Now let's go eat dessert."

He closed the door behind us.

LATER THAT evening, we all sat in the den watching *Meet Joe Black* on HBO. We had probably seen it a half dozen times already, but it was one of Grant's favorites.

Sometime early in the movie, Katy reached over and took my hand in hers—and I knew I was forgiven.

I leaned over and kissed her on top of her head. Whispered: "Thank you. I'm sorry."

She squeezed my hand. Whispered back: "No more secrets."

"Promise."

She rested her head on my shoulder.

Ten days later, I broke my promise.

✦✦✦

Saturday, Dec 21

THE MALL parking lot was a zoo. Grant carefully maneuvered his way around tired pedestrians overloaded with shopping bags and cranky, aggressive drivers looking for open parking spaces.

If there was an undercover cop following us today, he was impossible to spot in the long line of traffic behind us. *Or maybe they had given up,* I thought. It had, thankfully, been a quiet couple of days; even the press seemed to be taking a breather.

"Right there," I said, pointing at an SUV with its reverse lights on.

Grant flipped on his right turn signal and eased to a stop. The car behind us immediately blew its horn. I glanced in the passenger side mirror, but it was impossible to see because of the duct tape that was wrapped around it, keeping it attached to the car. The SUV backed out of the space, drove away, and we pulled in.

"Piece of cake," Grant said, smiling.

Our annual Christmas shopping trip had been a longstanding tradition—ever since Grant was in middle school and he'd started using his lawn mowing money to buy us gifts. Once he became old enough to drive, Grant had assumed chauffeuring duties for the day. It was usually an adventure.

"You know I could've driven today," I teased.

"Now what fun would that've been?"

I reached down and released my seat belt, and my hand brushed against something cold and metal between the seats. Concerned, I held up a wrench for Grant to see. "Ummm, protection? You worried about something, son?"

Grant just laughed and took the wrench from my hand. Without a word, he turned to the driver's door and used the wrench to hand-crank his window halfway open. I hadn't noticed until now that his window knob was missing. He looked back at me with a smirk, and then cranked the window closed again.

"Impressive," I said, shaking my head and climbing out of the old Subaru. "Mom's right. You *really* need a new car."

IF THE parking lot was a zoo, then the inside of the mall was a jungle. I had never seen that many people crammed into one space, except maybe at an Orioles game.

We had been shopping for over three hours and had purchased exactly two gifts. *Two*. How was that even possible?

On the plus side, it had been nice to have some alone time with Grant. We talked about school and life and football. We talked about my job and Katy; he agreed that her mood was brightening, and she was acting more like her old self every day. Having him home from college and a couple drama-free days had worked wonders for her.

And, of course, we talked about Jimmy. He told me about his ten-minute phone call with Detective Anderson before he'd left campus; she had been very nice to him, Grant said, for which I was grateful.

I'd had a scare early on when I thought I'd seen Jimmy watching us from behind a kiosk, but it turned out to be a false alarm. The guy was there with his grandchildren, pushing them around in one of those fancy double strollers. I saw him up close a short time later, and he didn't really resemble Jimmy at all.

WE ATE dinner in the food court, after a fifteen-minute wait in line for pizza and fries, and another five-minute wait for an open table. Afterward, when I came back from washing up in the bathroom, I saw a smiling Ken Ellis shaking hands with Grant.

"Here he is," Ken said, when he saw me approaching. "How's it hanging, Bobby?"

"Lot better once I get out of here," I said, glancing around at the throng of shoppers.

"Grant's looking good," he said, slapping my son on the back. "Big man on campus with the ladies, I'm sure."

Grant didn't say anything; just stood there looking embarrassed.

"Well, we better get going. Still need to buy a couple things and—"

Ken leaned in close. "Anything new about Wilkinson?"

I remembered what Katy had said: about Ken telling the cops that Jimmy and I were thick as thieves, and how he'd been spreading gossip around the neighborhood that maybe I was a suspect, too. I decided it was time for some payback.

I leaned in and lowered my voice. "No one is supposed to know this, not even the press, but..."

Ken's eyes widened. "But what?"

"The police...there's gonna be another big press conference tomorrow morning. 8am sharp. Right out front of the Fallston Police Department."

Ken's chubby, little face nodded up and down. "I knew there was more coming, I knew it." He looked around conspiratorially. "Thanks. I won't tell a soul." And he was gone.

Grant looked at me in surprise as we walked in the opposite direction. "Did you just do what I think you just did?"

"And what would that be?"

"You totally punked Mr. Ellis and sent him on a wild goose chase at eight in the morning."

I shrugged. "Karma's a bitch, son."

A FEW minutes later, browsing in a Barnes and Noble, Grant brought up the day he and Jimmy had spent in Gettysburg, walking the battlefield.

"It was probably my favorite day I ever spent with him," he told me.

I nodded. "I remember when you got home that night. You were so excited and couldn't wait to go to the library the next day to check out some books."

"I really loved walking around Gettysburg and learning about the battle, but it was more than that. I think it was because he treated me like a grown up for the first time that day. I was only fourteen, but the way he talked to me, the way he explained things...it made me feel special."

I knew what he meant. Jimmy had that way about him; a way of making you feel like the most important person in the world at any given moment.

"Something I've thought about a lot since all this happened..." He fidgeted with his jacket zipper, and I could tell he really wanted to get this out.

"When we were walking the field where General Pickett led his famous charge...he went on and on about the ghosts of the past and how he could feel their presence there on that battlefield. Each fallen soldier's hopes and dreams and fears and regrets. The way he described it...it gave me chills...and I swear it made me feel *something* there, too."

I nodded again, encouraging him to continue.

"The more you and Mom told me about what was happening...and the more I listened to the news reports...it really made me wonder what kind of ghosts Mr. Wilkinson has been carrying around with him all these years. I mean, if he did all the terrible things they claim he did... it's almost like there has to be another person inside of him...a ghost that none of us ever really knew..."

Sunday, Dec 22

THE MOOD was a lot lighter the next morning, as the three of us busied ourselves in the kitchen, getting ready for an afternoon of watching football with some of Grant's old high school friends.

A radiant Katy danced around the granite island, making her spicy pepperoni rolls and singing along with Elton John on the radio. Grant stirred a big pot of chili on the stove and cut up chicken wings on the counter. I sat at the breakfast bar, watching and laughing, as I peeled a bowl of jumbo steamed shrimp for pregame cocktails.

"I think we might need more wings," Grant said. "Mark and Tim are coming, and those boys can eat." He started rinsing his hands at the sink.

"You stay and finish. I'll go," I said.

Katy rolled her eyes. "The master escape artist gets out of doing his work yet again."

I plopped a fat shrimp in my mouth, chewed it up, and started talking with my mouth open. "Not true, Miss Know-It-All, and highly offensive. Grant needs to remain here in case his friends show up early. You know how they get when there's free food on the table."

They both laughed, and Katy shooed me out of the kitchen.

I WAS standing in line at the register with three packs of chicken wings and a family size bag of Doritos when my cell phone rang. I fumbled it out of my pocket, expecting it to be Katy asking me to pick up something else: chips or pretzels or maybe another jar of salsa.

Instead, the caller ID flashed a familiar message: *Unknown Caller.*

I answered, thinking: *No way it's him*. "Hello?"

I was wrong.

"I know they're tracking the call, so I have to be quick, Bobby. I've been thinking a lot about you and Katy and Grant. I just wanted to wish you all a Merry Christmas."

I didn't know what to say, so I didn't say anything.

"...and say how sorry I am again. You've been my one true friend, my entire life." The connection wasn't as clear as the first time. *Was he farther away?*

"Grant was like a son to me. I'm sorry to have put you all through this."

"You would never hurt us, right, Jimmy?" I asked, finally finding my voice.

A burst of static.

"Right?"

Another loud crackle of static, and was there something else? *Was he laughing?*

"Jimmy? Jimmy!"

The line went dead.

LATER THAT night in bed:

"I think we were right not to tell Grant," Katy said. "He was so happy today."

I handed her the television remote. "No reason to worry him over nothing."

"It's not nothing, Bobby." The look of wariness was back on her face.

"I didn't mean it that way."

"Are you sure he was laughing?"

"No, I'm not sure. I told you, there was too much static to hear clearly."

She placed the remote on the nightstand without turning on the television. "What time are you seeing Detective Anderson tomorrow?"

"I told her I'd come down to the station around ten."

"Do you want me to come with you? We could tell Grant we were running to the store."

I shook my head. "It's not necessary. Just stay home with him."

"Bobby?"

"Yeah, baby?"

"You swear you aren't hiding anything else from me?"

I leaned over and took her face in my hands. Looked into her eyes. "I promise you."

Monday, Dec 23

GRANT CAME downstairs after his morning shower, took one look at us sitting at the breakfast bar, and said, "What's wrong?"

I guess our faces gave it away.

The television was on: a Channel Eleven Special Report that had interrupted Katy's regular viewing of *Good Morning, America*.

The news wasn't good. Three more victims identified. Three more somber photographs of the deceased. Two women and a young man this time. Police sources described "souvenirs"—jewelry, articles of clothing, even a pair of driver's licenses—discovered beneath a floorboard in 1922 Hanson Road that had helped connect James Wilkinson to the murders.

Grant stood, arms crossed, and watched in silence; he looked as if he wanted to cry.

Katy got up and put a hand on his shoulder. "Honey..."

"That's *eight* now," he said, looking at her. "And they're saying there might be others."

"We just have to try to block it out. We have to try to—"

"Block it out?" he said, pulling away from her. "He was my Godfather for Christsake." Tears spilled from his eyes now. "I loved him."

"Grant—"

He waved her off and stormed out the side entrance into the garage, slamming the door behind him. Katy looked back at me with a helpless expression I had never before seen on her face.

"I'll go talk to him," I said.

BY THE time I entered the garage, the roll-up door was standing open, and Grant was nowhere to be found. I walked to the bottom of the driveway and searched in both directions. A garbage truck was turning the corner at the intersection. Otherwise, the street was empty and silent. Not even the sound of a passing car or a dog barking somewhere in the distance. The morning air was bracingly cold; I could see my breath in front of my face. Grant's hair had been wet from his shower. He'd only been wearing jeans and a t-shirt.

Where in the world had he gone off to?

"HE OBVIOUSLY feels very strongly about you," Detective Anderson said.

We were sitting in the same dinghy interview room as the last time I had been at the station. The same camera was recording our conversation.

"He knows we're watching you and tracing your calls, yet he still risked contact."

"He sounded sad and lonely. It's Christmas."

"We have someone trying to clean up the audio right now. Do you really believe he was laughing at the end of the phone call?"

"I don't know. For one second, I thought maybe I could hear him, but it was probably just static."

"Have you ever considered that he might be playing a game with you, Mr. Howard?"

"Why would he do that?"

"Why would he torture, mutilate, and kill at least eight innocent people?"

I had no answer for that.

"You told me once that Mr. Wilkinson likes to play chess. We found several other strategy-based games downloaded on his laptop."

"Okay…"

"We also found a hidden collection of video tapes in his garage. It seems Mr. Wilkinson was stalking and filming some of his victims ahead of time. At their homes. Work. The grocery store."

I felt my jaw tighten. "Why are you telling me this?"

"Because I think it's important that you realize a couple things about James Wilkinson: he is very smart, and he likes his games."

"Okay. I'm hearing you."

"Anything else at all you can think to share? It's important you tell me, no matter how small or trivial you might consider it."

I shook my head. "Nothing."

She stared directly at me. "And you would never keep anything from us, right?"

I almost said *You sound like my wife*, but held it in. Thank God. "No, I wouldn't."

"Still think you have nothing to worry about, Mr. Howard?"

She was looking for a reaction, and she got one.

"Do I think Jimmy would hurt us? No, I don't. Do I want you to find him and put him away? Yes, I do." Deep breath. "Look, he was my friend. A part of my family. And, yeah, he has the same name as my brother, but that doesn't mean a damn thing in the big picture. It's hard to think about everything we shared—Christ, just three weeks ago, he sat at my table and carved our Thanksgiving turkey—and it's even harder to think that none of it was real. But it wasn't. I know that. None of it was real."

"Well, it's good to hear you say that, Mr. Howard. Because it appears that he isn't quite finished yet. Last night, Pennsylvania police discovered a local florist murdered in her home and her car missing. They believe that James Wilkinson is responsible."

IT WASN'T real.

The words echoed in my head the entire drive home from the police station. I suddenly felt so tired. Beaten.

None of it was real.

I thought about all the times we had talked about the meaning of life and death; if there was a God or not; a heaven or a hell awaiting us; all of Jimmy's Army stories; the laughter-filled conversations about history and politics and football and the Orioles.

I thought about the countless times he'd helped me with odd jobs around the house and how he was the one who'd taught me how to use half the tools in my garage. The time he loaned me money so I could afford to send Grant to summer camp. And the time he counseled—and talked sense into—me after I confided in him that I was thinking about having an affair with a co-worker; my solitary near-slip in over twenty years of a happy marriage.

And I remembered the night, just the two of us sitting out back on the deck, watching a meteor shower, when he put his beer down and turned to me and said:

"Whatever you do, don't ever lie to yourself, Bobby. People lie to themselves all the time. To survive. To get by. But you look those people in the eyes—even the toughest of the bunch—and you ask them, 'What do you think about when you see a shooting star in the night sky? Better yet, *who* do you think about?' Because that right there is their truth, and in that moment even they can't deny it. Maybe the saddest thing of all is those same people are usually the ones who stop watching stars that fall from the sky. They can't handle their own truths, so they learn to just turn away from the magic."

It was beautiful and poetic and maybe the wisest thing anyone had ever said to me.

And none of it was real.

✦✦✦

Tuesday, Dec 24

SURPRISINGLY, CHRISTMAS Eve turned out to be a wonderful day for all of us.

Despite the grisly news reports about Jimmy, and my trip downtown to the police station the day before—Channel Eleven aired parking lot footage of both my arrival and departure from the stationhouse—it was almost as if the three of us had made an unspoken agreement to wake up fresh and clear-headed and not allow any of the chaos to interfere with us properly celebrating the holiday.

Katy and I had been worried at first. After disappearing for nearly two hours the day before—and offering no explanation upon his return—Grant had spent most of the afternoon and evening hidden away in his bedroom with the door closed and had barely spoken a word to us at dinner. This morning, he'd slept in late, and we'd feared that he was still hanging onto those dark feelings.

But then he'd shocked us by bounding down the stairs a few minutes past eleven, a smile on his face, starving for a big breakfast and already dressed to go Christmas tree shopping.

When Grant was still living at home, we would always pick out our family tree the first weekend of December and set it up that Sunday evening. Now, that he was away at college, it had become tradition to buy it on Christmas Eve morning and set it up after dinner and a nighttime walk around the neighborhood to look at Christmas lights.

We'd decided to skip the walk this year—after a quick discussion confirmed that none of us were particularly anxious to see or talk to any of our neighbors—but dinner had been amazing, as usual (Katy's homemade lasagna, rolls, and salad), and the tree took us until almost nine o'clock to finish decorating.

We'd watched the end of *White Christmas* on television, and then hugged Grant goodnight as he went up to bed. Once we were sure he was asleep, Katy and I had made love on the sofa in the comforting glow of the Christmas tree and dozed in each other's arms afterward.

For just a moment, everything had felt okay again in the world.

I LISTENED to Katy's footsteps climbing the stairs and finished rinsing our wine glasses in the sink. I turned off the kitchen lights and returned to the den to close-up.

I couldn't take my eyes off the Christmas tree. It's twinkling lights and wintergreen smell brought back so many nostalgic memories. Grant, as a young boy, leaving cookies and milk and a handwritten note on the mantle for Santa; a pile of chopped-up carrots on the floor for his reindeer. Katy and I sneaking presents under the tree once we were certain that Grant had fallen asleep. Both of us embracing a carefree and innocent world where little boys and girls believed in magic and Santa Claus was real.

I bent to a knee and rehung an angel ornament that had shaken loose and tumbled down through the branches—and another memory washed over me.

Every Christmas Eve as boys, after evening mass, my brother and I would walk hand in hand to the top of Tupelo Drive. Once we'd reached the crest of the hill, we would stand at the crossroad and look down Juniper Street at the carnival of twinkling lights decorating the houses along both sides of the road. Jimmy always used to say that it was like our own personal Christmas parade—and he was right.

After taking our time strolling down Juniper, Jimmy and I would return home to change into pajamas, drink Mom's hot cocoa, and open one early Christmas present each. Then Mom would tuck us in, and we would whisper back and forth to each other across our cramped bedroom until we finally fell asleep.

It was the clearest and most favorite memory I had of my brother—and it filled my soul and made my heart ache, all at once.

I unplugged the Christmas tree lights and walked upstairs in darkness.

Wednesday, Dec 25

I GAWKED at the huge present wrapped in *Frosty the Snowman* gift paper. "I have *no* idea what it is!"

"And that's enough to drive you crazy, isn't it?" Katy beamed.

Grant laughed, and high-fived his mother.

"Whatever," I said, sounding very much like a pouting child.

I was notoriously difficult to surprise when it came to gifts, and that was somewhat of an understatement. If constant badgering—*"What'd you get me? What'd you get me? C'mon, just give me a hint."*—didn't work, then I usually resorted to sneaking around the house, searching high and low for hidden caches of presents or store receipts.

One year, I even snuck downstairs and used an exacto knife to carefully slice open the wrapping paper of one of my gifts under the tree. Once I had determined the gift's identity, I'd used scotch tape to carefully reseal it.

I would have gotten away with it, too, if it hadn't been for Katy being such a light sleeper. Suffice to say, she no longer put presents under the tree until late on Christmas Eve night.

"Go ahead, open it," she said, still grinning.

I didn't have to be told twice. I tore open the wrapping paper with a couple quick swipes of my hands. My mouth dropped open.

"A snow-blower!" I tilted the box for a better look at it, and then gave Katy a big thank you hug and kiss. I couldn't stop smiling.

"Well, well, better write it down on the calendar, folks. Bobby Howard has finally been surprised!"

Still smiling, I slid a small gift out of the pocket of my flannel pjs. Handed it to Katy.

"What's this?"

"You're not the only one who likes surprises." I looked at Grant and winked.

Katy slowly unwrapped—*My god, who takes their time opening Christmas presents?!*—the narrow box and lifted the lid. A string of pearls shined like miniature angels in the rays of morning sunshine coming through the bay windows.

She held them up in one hand and put the other hand to her mouth. "Oh…oh…oh my God…" And then she squealed and practically tackled me in a bear hug.

"Mark those calendars again, folks. Katy Howard has just been rendered—surely for the first time ever in her life—speechless."

And then it was my turn to laugh and high-five Grant.

AFTER THE three of us fawned over our gifts some more—Grant was especially enamored with his new iPad Pro—and cleaned up the wrapping paper mess on the floor, we had just enough time to enjoy bagels and coffee and get dressed before Katy's parents arrived for the day.

Her parents were *never* late, and today was no exception. Within minutes of their arrival, Katy's mom was buzzing around the kitchen, helping with dinner preparations, and her father was camped out in front of the television in my recliner with his shoes off. The smell of Old Spice cologne was overwhelming.

A short time later, Katy's sister, Anne, and her husband and two little girls arrived from Ohio. We had kept their trip a secret from Katy's parents, so after a brief and tearful reunion, we all retreated to the den for an afternoon of catching up, food, college football, food, board games, food, more gift opening, and more food.

The only time I heard Jimmy's name was during a local, television newsbreak at halftime of one of the football games. Pennsylvania State Police had arrested a former employee for the murder of the florist. Here in Maryland, a trucker thought he'd spotted Jimmy driving a late model Mustang on I-95 south of Baltimore, but he'd been unable to get a license plate. And that was it—then it was back to football.

By seven o'clock, I felt more like a stuffed Thanksgiving turkey than a Christmas elf. I dozed at the end of the sofa; my swollen belly hidden beneath a pillow.

By nine o'clock, Katy's parents had left for home and her sister and family had gone back to their hotel for the night. We were alone again, and happily exhausted.

KATY WALKED into the bathroom as I was brushing my teeth. I rinsed my mouth and spit into the sink. "Today was nice, wasn't it?"

"Today was perfect." She lifted herself up on tiptoes and kissed me on the cheek. "Thank you."

"You're welcome, honey. Thank *you*."

Another kiss, this time on the mouth. "Can I ask you something?"

"Of course."

"Should I feel guilty reacting the way I did to your surprise this morning?"

I looked at her, confused.

"I mean, with everything going on. Jimmy. The poor families of the victims. And I got so excited and happy..."

I took her gently by the shoulders. "No, no, no, you should *not* feel guilty, and either should I. We've worked hard to get where we are. We deserve to be happy once in a while."

"Okay, good," she said, and I could tell she was relieved.

I walked into the bedroom and climbed under the covers. "It was nice to see your mom and dad today. They were actually a little calmer than I thought they'd be."

"They've both stopped watching the news and reading the newspaper. That's helped a lot."

"Mark offered to lend me a gun, can you believe that?" Mark was our brother-in-law, an avid hunter and outdoorsman.

"I hope you told him no," she said above the water running in the bathroom.

"Of course, I did. Told him I'd probably shoot myself in the dick the first time I tried to use it."

Katy laughed and turned off the water. "Well, I'm glad you told him that," she said, appearing in the doorway wearing her new string of pearls—and nothing else. "Because I really like your dick."

She turned off the light and came to bed.

FRIDAY, DEC 27

"THERE YOU are," Grant said from inside the garage.

I was kneeling at the top of the driveway, trying to assemble my new snow-blower. It was slow going, parts scattered everywhere, and I couldn't help but think about Jimmy and how he would usually be the one helping me do this.

"Mom wants to stop by the mall to return the sweater Grandma gave her—of course—and then we're meeting Uncle Mark and the girls at Chili's for lunch. You wanna come?"

I stood and brushed dirt from my jeans. "Sure. Give me ten minutes to finish here and wash up."

He glanced at the mess I had made and flashed me a skeptical look.

"Okay, okay, maybe twenty. But they're calling for snow tomorrow night, and I want to be ready."

"I'll tell Mom a half-hour," Grant said with a big shit-eating grin and walked back inside.

"Nobody likes a smartass," I called after him, and just like that, I was blindsided by an unexpected surge of fatherly love and pride. For reasons I couldn't even begin to explain, I felt sudden tears sting my eyes.

A dog barked on the street behind me, and I turned around just in time to see my neighbor, Aaron, picking up his newspaper and walking into his garage with his old German Shepard, Sarge, in tow.

I wiped a tear from my eye and walked down the driveway to my own newspaper box. I needed a moment to compose myself.

I grabbed the rolled-up newspaper from inside the box and opened it while I walked back to the house.

Halfway up the driveway, I stopped in my tracks, my heart skipping a beat. I stood perfectly still, the rest of the world melting away to nothing around me and stared down at the paper. I read the words again, slower this time.

Then, I carefully refolded the newspaper and slid it into my back pocket—and went inside.

Sunday, Dec 29

IT WAS just after midnight, and I was sneaking out of the house like a teenager.

Katy and Grant had been asleep for almost an hour, and the house was dark and silent. Snow was falling outside and had already blanketed the lawns and streets. The forecast called for six to nine inches by morning.

Dressed in dark pants and sweatshirt, I crept down the stairs, made my way through the den, and out the kitchen door into the garage.

I grabbed a heavy jacket and Grant's keys from the workbench, where I had left them earlier in the evening, slipped into my freezing cold boots, and eased open the door to the side yard.

Snow and wind lashed my face and threatened to yank the door from my hand. I tightened my grip and carefully pushed the door closed. If the wind had slammed it shut and awakened Katy, I was a dead man with an awful lot of explaining to do.

I marched around the side yard, through a couple inches of fresh snow, to the driveway and Grant's Subaru. I would have much preferred to take my own car or even Katy's, but Grant's car was parked in its usual spot, blocking the garage door, and with snow in the forecast, I hadn't been able to think of a single good excuse to ask Grant to park in the street. Not without raising suspicion.

I had spent the past thirty-six hours doing my best to not raise any suspicions, and it had been an exhausting task. Saturday had passed like an eternity. So many thoughts ricocheting around inside my head—and heart—and I had changed my mind a half-dozen times before finally settling on my decision.

I used my bare hands to clear away snow from the Subaru's windshield, then climbed inside and eased the door closed. The interior of the car smelled like old pizza and dirty socks. I inserted the key in the ignition, unlocked the steering wheel, put the car in neutral, and released the parking brake.

Holding my breath, I drifted silently down the driveway and into the snow-covered street. The slope of Hanson Road carried me most of the way clear of my house, and only then did I attempt to crank the engine.

It wheezed and sputtered several times before finally catching. I strapped on my seatbelt and drove carefully out of the neighborhood.

At least this piece of junk has four-wheel drive, I thought, turning right onto Edgewood Road and cruising past the all-night Dunkin' Donuts and Texaco station.

THE NOTE had been hidden in the Friday morning edition of the *Baltimore Sun*.

Tucked away in the SPORTS section, it had been scribbled on a sheet of torn-out notebook paper, and I had recognized the handwriting before I'd even had time to digest the contents of the note.

After I'd read it the first couple times in the driveway, I'd hidden the note in the pocket of my jeans and read it twice more at the mall when Katy and Grant had been off on their own. I'd read it again a short time later in the bathroom stall at Chili's.

Later that Friday evening, after everyone had gone upstairs, I'd read the note one final time—and then I'd burned it in the fireplace. Once I was certain there was nothing left but ashes, I'd gone upstairs to bed and lay awake for hours.

THE STREETS were empty—except for the occasional snow-plow lurking past me like some kind of prehistoric monster—and once I hit Route 22, I was surprised by how quickly I got there.

Not even twenty minutes after drifting down my driveway, I slowed and pulled to the side of the road—at the exact spot where Jimmy and I had once chased a baby deer into the woods, laughing and carrying on like teenagers without a care in the world. It seemed like a lifetime ago, now.

I swung around and did a U-turn, so the car would be parked on the correct side of the road, and as I did, my headlights swept across a snow-covered field, exposing a staggered line of boot prints in an otherwise pristine blanket of fresh powder. The prints disappeared into the distant treeline.

I OWE YOU ONE FINAL TRUTH, BOBBY. PLEASE MEET ME.

I adjusted and zipped up my heavy jacket. Pulled on a winter hat. Took a couple deep breaths to calm myself. Then turned off the car and got out.

The snow was coming down harder now, the flakes fatter and wetter, and the wind had picked up. I adjusted my jacket collar and stuffed my hands into my pockets.

SUNDAY. 12:30AM. BABY DEER WOODS. I HAVE SOMETHING I NEED TO GIVE YOU BEFORE I GO AWAY FOREVER.

I started across the field, following the quickly disappearing boot tracks in the snow. I felt bulky and sluggish, like an overdressed snowman. The wind slowed my pace even more and stung my eyes. I squeezed them shut for a moment and saw Lisa James's bloodied face—just as she had been appearing in my nightly dreams—the seventeen-year-old, Dartmouth-bound beauty who had been killed in the utility shed at her swimming pool.

PLEASE MEET ME, BOBBY. PLEASE DON'T BE AFRAID. I WOULD NEVER HURT YOU.

That's right, Bob, nothing at all to be afraid of, I thought, as I lowered my head and kept on walking.

Hell, I wasn't afraid. I was scared shitless.

I CROSSED a frozen creek, using ice-slippery rocks as a pathway, and slowly stepped into the woods, my eyes moving everywhere. Most of the wind was blocked here, but it moaned even louder high above me in the treetops. It took my eyes a moment to adjust to the darkness.

"Jimmy?" My voice sounded like a stranger's.

I walked deeper into the woods. It felt like I was watching someone else in a movie. Someone very scared and foolish.

"Jimmy?"

I thought I heard the snap of dead branches to my right, and I stopped moving, holding my breath and listening.

"That you, Jimmy?"

Nothing, but the wind.

I started walking again, and—

"I'm right here, Bobby."

From directly behind me.

✦✦✦

I JERKED like I'd been hit with a taser and spun around—and there he was, my old friend.

Standing next to the tree I had just walked past.

He was wearing dark pants and a sweatshirt with the hood up. No jacket. I couldn't see his eyes and could see just enough of the rest of his face to tell that he hadn't shaved in a long time. I had never seen him with a beard. He looked like someone I'd never laid eyes on before, which I guess was the point.

"I didn't mean to scare you, Bobby."

We were standing maybe fifteen feet apart.

"No big deal. Just ruined a brand new pair of underwear. I can throw them away when I get home."

Jimmy laughed, and I hated that the sound of it made my heart feel something. "Same ole Bobby. God, it's good to see you."

He took a step forward, but I held my hands up to stop him. "That's close enough...please."

Jimmy froze, and I watched his shoulders sag. "I'm not going to hurt you. I would never do that, Bobby."

"I told the police that. They didn't believe me, either did Katy, but I told them."

"I guess you can't really blame them. I've done some terrible things."

And there it was—an admission.

Wasn't that what I'd come for?

"Why, Jimmy?"

Jimmy lowered his head, and I saw his chest rise and fall. "It's like I already told you, I couldn't help it." He looked up at me again, and his face was sick with the truth of it. "It's a compulsion...a sickness...a kind of fever...I fight it as hard as I can and I win for a while...but then it comes back and I'm weak again..."

He inched closer to me while he was talking, and I suddenly heard Detective Anderson's words inside my head: *He likes to play games, Mr. Howard.*

"I have something I need to give to you, Bobby." Another step closer, and his hand disappeared into his sweatshirt pocket. "Something very special."

I took a careful step backward, hoping he wouldn't notice—and prayed that the snipers could see well enough in the dark and falling snow to have a clear shot.

I DIDN'T know where the snipers were positioned, only that there were three of them, and they had set up hours ago, well before Jimmy was supposed to have arrived. I was wired under my sweatshirt and had a safe word, and they were supposed to be watching and listening to my every move.

Of course, my overactive and terrified imagination informed me that there was always the possibility that Jimmy had ambushed the snipers, and the three of them were hanging upside down from trees right now, gutted like deer, their steaming blood staining the snow red.

I forced myself to ignore that awful imagery and took another half-step back.

"Your family is the only family I ever had, Bobby. Being with you and Katy and Grant is the only time I ever felt safe or happy in my entire, miserable life."

Jimmy walked closer.

"That's what makes this so damn difficult…"

He pulled something long and white from his pocket.

I HAD spent the second half of Friday and all of Saturday wrestling with my decision: tell Detective Anderson about the note or keep it to myself?

By Saturday evening—an early goodbye dinner at the house for Anne and her family—I had decided to keep the note to myself and not go to meet Jimmy. I didn't know if it was the right decision, only that it felt like the safest and least complicated action I could take for my family.

And I was at peace with that choice—until the phone call.

Detective Anderson rung the house phone just as dinner was winding down, and I'd excused myself, hurrying upstairs to take the call in the bedroom.

"I'm sorry to interrupt your dinner, Mr. Howard. This won't take very long."

I paced back and forth in front of the bed, suddenly nervous that she had somehow discovered the note—and my failure to disclose it. "It's okay. How can I help you?"

"Just two questions and you can get back to eating. Does a woman named Janie Loughlin work for you?"

"Janie? Umm, yeah, but technically she works *with* me, not for me."

"Is Ms. Loughlin an acquaintance of Mr. Wilkinson's?"

I stopped pacing. "Not really. I mean, they've met a couple times. At cookouts here at the house. And Jimmy came to our office Christmas party once or twice over the years."

"Do you know if the two of them had remained in any kind of contact with each other?"

"I don't think so. I think Jimmy would have said something if they had, and I *know* Janie would have. Why are you asking me this?"

There was a brief moment of silence on the phone, then: "I told you about the videotapes Mr. Wilkinson had made of some of his victims. The most recent batch of tapes we discovered included nearly three hours of footage of Janie Loughlin performing a variety of activities ranging from walking her dogs in the park to gardening in her side yard to entering and leaving your office building."

I sat down on the edge of the bed.

"I think it's safe to say that Ms. Loughlin is a very fortunate woman."

I leaned over and rested my face in my hands.

"But just in case, we've gone ahead and assigned her around-the-clock protection."

I didn't say anything. I couldn't.

"Mr. Howard? Are you still there? Mr. Howard?"

I finally sat up. Cleared my throat. "There's something I need to tell you, detective, but you have to promise not to tell Katy..."

DEAD BRANCHES crunching beneath his boots, Jimmy edged closer in the dark woods, and I knew I had maybe two seconds to make a choice. I felt my legs tense, but they remained frozen in place.

"I'm so sorry, Bobby." He reached out with a shaking hand—and I saw that he was holding a crumpled, white envelope.

He held it out toward me—*"Be careful, he likes to play games, Mr. Howard"*—and I took it, backing away once I had it in my hand.

The envelope was sealed. I shook it, and something heavy rattled inside. "What is it?"

"It's...something that belongs to you."

I didn't want to open the envelope.

Somehow, I knew that whatever secrets it held inside would forever change my life, and I didn't want to open it and find out.

But, of course, I had to.

I turned the envelope over in my hand, once, twice, then tore it open along the top. I tilted the envelope and something small and metal slid out into my open palm. I held it up in front of my face—and suddenly I couldn't remember how to breathe. My vision blurred.

It was a miniature lightning bolt pendant hanging on a faded silver chain. The same one my brother had been wearing on the day he disappeared.

AS I'D grown older, I had learned to tell people that my brother, Jimmy, had drowned for two simple reasons: first, because that was the most likely explanation for his disappearance. Lake Codorus was dark and deep, and people—kids and adults, alike—drowned in its waters at the rate of once every two or three years. It wasn't a terribly rare occurrence, merely a tragic one.

The second reason was because it was simply easier. I could have explained that the body had never been found, and that the police had also conducted an extensive missing person's investigation, and that the investigation had turned up no evidence of foul play; but that would have just led to even more questions and extended a conversation in which I loathed to take part in the first place. If there was one thing I'd learned growing up, it was this: people couldn't shut up and mind their own business when it came to a genuine real-life mystery. They all turned into amateur detectives.

So, as the years passed, by default, it had become the official explanation: James Alvin Howard had drowned in Lake Codorus at the age of thirteen.

Only now I knew better.

"YOU..." MY legs felt like they might give out. I staggered back a step, regained my balance. "You killed him?"

Jimmy nodded and lowered his head.

"Answer the fucking question. You killed him?"

"Yes." Barely audible above the wind.

I felt like I was going to faint. "How? That was...almost forty years ago."

Jimmy looked up at me, and this time I could see his eyes. I wish I could say that they looked dead or empty, like a shark's eyes; I wish I could say that they didn't look human; that they looked like a monster's eyes.

But that wouldn't have been the truth.

He looked very much like my old friend right then, standing there in front of me in the snowy woods, his eyes sadder and more tired than I had ever seen a person's eyes look before or since.

He cleared his throat and started talking:

"I had just turned twenty the month before and was on a two-week leave from the Army. Most of my buddies had gone home or to the beach for some R&R and women, but I had taken off on a solo road trip instead. Mom was dead by then, so I had nobody, and nowhere to go.

"I'd driven south, and that's how I ended up at your lake on my second day out. At first, I'd just laid out and read a book on the beach and got some sun, drank some beers from a cooler I'd brought along; but then I saw your brother splashing around in the lake...and he looked so young and alive...and I felt something."

"*Something*?"

He flexed his hands in front of him. "An urge…an itch…down in the deepest and darkest part of my brain. I knew what I was feeling, and I fought it. I even loaded up my stuff in the car and left. But a few miles down the road, I turned around."

"And you went back. He was…the first one?"

"No." He shook his head. "The second."

"Who was the—"

"My sister didn't die from cancer, Bobby. She was real sick and she probably would have died soon anyway…but she didn't die from cancer."

It was too much; I felt something breaking open inside of me. "So, all these years…"

"I followed the story in the news and the papers. I learned all about the sweet single mom who had lost her older son to the lake, and I learned all about the younger son still with her. The guilt and regret ate away at me. I tried to think of ways to make it up to the two of you…"

"Make it up to us?" I asked, incredulous.

"I was sick, Bobby. My brain wasn't working right. Even, years later, when I couldn't fight it anymore and I started killing again, I still thought about you and felt guilty about what I'd done. I did my best to keep track of you as you grew up. I kept a scrapbook. Newspaper clippings from back in high school about your baseball games and your business scholarship. Some of the guest editorials you wrote for your college newspaper. An interview you did for the alumni newsletter when you were working your first job. Even your wedding announcement to Katy.

"A lot of time went by, but I never forgot about you, Bobby. I couldn't. And then one night, maybe ten years ago, not long after my wife passed away, I was living in New Jersey, and I had an idea. I knew it was a crazy idea, but I couldn't stop thinking about it: what if I found out where you were living and became a part of your neighborhood; a part of your *life*?"

"All this time…"

Jimmy nodded. "All this time…I didn't know what I'd thought would happen, even after I moved in right next door to you. But I never dreamed it would turn out like this. I never dreamed I would learn to love you and trust you. Like a brother."

"Don't you fucking say that!"

He put his hands up. "I'm sorry. I didn't mean to—"

"Why tell me all this now?"

"I *always* wanted to tell you, Bobby. Not a single day passed that I didn't think about it. I wrote about it in my journal all the time. But when all this happened and I had to run away...I knew that if I didn't tell you now, if I didn't find a way to return the necklace to you, you would probably never find out." He almost seemed to shrink in size in front of me. "I just thought you should know...no matter how much it made you hate me."

I took a step closer to him.

"What happened to my brother, Jimmy?"

He glanced at the ground. "When I got back to the lake, I watched and waited until he went to the restroom alone, and then I tricked him into helping me with my car in the parking lot. The whole thing took maybe three minutes, and we were gone."

My brain felt like it was on fire. "What...did you do to him?"

He looked at me. "I'm not going to tell you that, Bobby. I can't."

"Where's my brother, Jimmy? What'd you do with his body?"

"I buried what was left of..." He caught himself, quickly looked away from me again. "I buried him deep in the forest, up past Harrisburg National Park."

What was left of him...what was left of him...what was...

Whatever control I had left abandoned me then—and I pulled the wrench I had snuck out of Grant's Subaru from my coat pocket and smashed Jimmy across his face with it.

I felt his cheek and nose explode, and he collapsed hard to the ground, blood spurting.

It was hard to move with the bulletproof vest Detective Anderson had insisted I wear, but I lunged forward and was on top of Jimmy before he could get up.

Hitting him...again and again and again...until he wasn't moving anymore, and the wrench was slick with blood and clumps of hair.

He likes to play games, Mr. Howard.

But, even then, I didn't stop, I couldn't stop smashing what was left of his face, over and over again—

—until suddenly Detective Anderson and the other cops were there next to me, barking orders in my face and pulling me off of him.

And then the woods all around me were alive with voices and footsteps, and there was nothing left for me to do but lay there sprawled on my back in the trampled snow, staring up at the uncaring December sky, as one cop read Jimmy his rights—*"I don't think he's gonna need those, Dan."*—and another cop radioed in for an ambulance; and then a helicopter buzzed the treetops overhead, its spotlight cutting through the skeletal branches, bathing us in its circle of golden light, the snow falling harder now all around us, looking like angel tears sifting down through the heavenly glow; and then my shattered mind had just enough time to think—*Isn't it so beautiful? Like we're inside one of Katy's snow globes...*—before Detective Anderson was kneeling at my side, taking me into her arms—*"Hurry, he's going into shock!"*—and even then I couldn't stop, I couldn't stop sobbing his name: "JIMMYYYY!"

Over and over again.

Only to be drowned out by the roar of the helicopter overhead.

A FACE IN THE CROWD

STEPHEN KING
STEWART O'NAN

DISCARD

CEMETERY DANCE PUBLICATIONS

Baltimore

❖ 2023 ❖

PACIFIC GROVE PUBLIC LIBRARY
550 CENTRAL AVENUE
PACIFIC GROVE, CA 93950
(831) 648-5760

A Face in the Crowd

Copyright © 2023 by Stephen King and Stewart O'Nan
Cemetery Dance Publications special edition

All rights reserved. No part of this book may be reproduced in any form or by any electronic or mechanical means, including information storage and retrieval systems, without permission in writing from the publisher, except by a reviewer who may quote brief passages in a review.

Cemetery Dance Publications
132B Industry Lane, Unit #7
Forest Hill, MD 21050
www.cemeterydance.com

The characters and events in this book are fictitious. Any similarity to real persons, living or dead, is coincidental and not intended by the author.

First Cemetery Dance Printing

ISBN: 978-1-58767-822-6

Cover Artwork and Design © 2023 by François Vaillancourt
Cover and Interior Design © 2023 by Desert Isle Design, LLC
Interior Artwork © 2023 by Mark Edward Geyer

THE SUMMER AFTER HIS WIFE DIED, Dean Evers started watching a lot of baseball. Like so many snowbirds from New England, he was a Red Sox fan who'd fled the nor'easters for the Gulf Coast of Florida and magnanimously adopted the Devil Rays, then perennial punching-bags, as his second team. While he'd coached little league, he'd never been a big fan—never obsessed, the way his son Pat was—but, night after night, as the gaudy sunset colored the west, he found himself turning on the Rays game to fill his empty condo.

He knew it was just a way of passing time. He and Ellie had been married forty-six years, through the good and the bad, and now he had no one who remembered any of it. She was the one who'd lobbied him to move to St. Pete, and then, not five years after they packed up the house, she had her stroke. The terrible thing was that she was in great shape. They'd just played a bracing set of tennis at the club. She'd beat him again, meaning he bought the drinks. They were sitting under an umbrella, sipping chilled gin-and-tonics, when she winced and pressed a hand over one eye.

"Brain freeze?" he asked.

She didn't move, sat there stuck, her other eye fixed, staring far beyond him.

"El," he said, reaching to touch her bare shoulder. Later, though the doctor said it was impossible, he would remember her skin being cold.

She folded face-first onto the table, scattering their glasses, bringing the waiters and the manager and the lifeguard from the pool, who gently laid her head on a folded towel and knelt beside her, monitoring her pulse until the EMTs arrived. She lost everything on her right side, but she was alive, that was what mattered, except, quickly, not a month after she finished her PT and came home from the rehab, she had a second, fatal stroke while he was giving her a shower, a scene which replayed in his mind so often that he decided he had to move to a new place, which brought him here, to a bayside high-rise where he knew no one and anything that helped pass the time was welcome.

He ate while he watched the game. He made his own dinner now, having tired of eating alone in restaurants and ordering expensive takeout. He was still learning the basics. He could make pasta and grill a steak, cut up a red pepper to crown a bag salad. He had no finesse, and too often was discouraged at the results, taking little pleasure in them. Tonight was a pre-seasoned pork chop he'd picked up at the Publix. Just stick it in a hot pan and go, except he could never tell when meat was done. He got the chop crackling, threw a salad together and set a place at the coffee table, facing the TV. The fat at the bottom of the pan was beginning to char. He poked the meat with a finger, testing for squishiness, but couldn't be sure. He took a knife and cut into it, revealing a pocket of blood. The pan was going to be hell to clean.

And then, when he finally sat down and took his first bite, the chop was tough. "Terrible," he heckled himself. "Chef Ramsay you ain't."

The Rays were playing the Mariners, meaning the stands were empty. When the Sox or Yanks were in town, the Trop was packed, otherwise the place was deserted. In the bad old days it made sense, but now the club was a serious contender. As David Price breezed through the lineup, Evers noted with dismay several fans in the padded captain's chairs behind the plate talking on their cellphones. Inevitably, one teenager began waving like a castaway, presumably to the person on the other end, watching at home.

"Look at me," Evers said. "I'm on TV, therefore I exist."

The kid waved for several pitches. He was right over the umpire's shoulder, and when Price dropped in a backdoor curve, the replay zoomed on the Met Life strike zone, magnifying the kid's idiotic grin as he waved in slow motion. Two rows behind him, sitting alone in his white sanitary smock with his thin, pomaded hair slicked back, solid and stoic as a tiki god, was Evers's old dentist from Shrewsbury, Dr. Young.

Young Dr. Young, his mother had called him, because even when Evers was a child, he'd been old. He'd been a Marine in the Pacific, had come back from Tarawa missing part of a leg and all of his hope. He'd spent the rest of his life exacting his revenge not on the Japanese but on the children of Shrewsbury, finding soft spots in their enamel with the pitiless point of his stainless steel hook and plunging needles into their gums.

Evers stopped chewing and leaned forward to be sure. The greased-back hair and Mount Rushmore forehead, the Coke bottle bifocals and thin lips that went white when he bore down with the drill—yes, it was him, and not a day older than when Evers had last seen him, over fifty years ago.

It couldn't be. He'd be at least ninety. But the humidor that was Florida was full of men his age, many of them well-preserved, near-mummified beneath their guayaberas and tans.

No, Evers thought, he'd smoked. It was another thing Evers hated about him, the stale reek of his breath and his clothes as he loomed in close over him, trying to get leverage. The red pack fit the pocket of his smock—Lucky Strikes, filterless, the true coffin nails. *L.S.M.F.T.*, that was the old slogan: *Lucky Strike Means Fine Tobacco.* Perhaps it was a younger brother, or a son. Even Younger Dr. Young.

Price blew a fastball by the batter to end the inning and a commercial intervened, hauling Evers back to the present. His porkchop was tough as a catcher's mitt. He tossed it in the trash and grabbed a beer. The first cold gulp sobered him. There was no way that was his Dr. Young, with his shaky morning-after hands and more than a hint of gin under his cigarette breath. Nowadays they'd call his condition PTSD, but to a kid at the mercy of his instruments, it didn't matter. Evers had despised him, had surely at some point wished him, if not dead, then gone.

When the Rays came to bat, the teenager was waving again, but the rows behind him were vacant. Evers kept an eye out, expecting Dr. Young to come back with a beer and a hot dog, yet as the innings passed and Price's strikeouts mounted, the seat remained empty. Nearby, a woman in a sparkly top was now waving to the folks at home.

He wished Ellie were there to tell, or that he could call his mother and ask whatever happened to Young Dr. Young, but, as with so much of his daily existence, there was no one to share it with. More likely than not, the man was just another old guy with nothing better to do than waste his leftover evenings watching baseball, only at the park instead of at home.

Late that night, around three, Evers could easily see why of all the possible punishments prisoners feared solitary confinement the most. At some point a beating had to stop, but a thought could go on and on, feeding and then feeding on insomnia. Why Dr. Young, who he hadn't thought of in years? Was it a sign? An omen? Or was he—as he feared he might when they told him Ellie had died—gradually losing his grip on this world?

To prove those doubts wrong, he spent the next day running errands around town, chatting with the clerk at the post office, and the woman at the circulation desk of the library—just small talk, but still, a connection, something to build on. Like every summer, Pat and his family had taken off for the Cape and Sue's folks' place. Evers called their machine anyway and left a message. When they came back they should really get together. He'd love to take them all out to dinner somewhere, their choice, or maybe a ballgame.

That evening he prepared his dinner as if nothing had happened, though now he was very aware of the time, and ended up rushing his grilled chicken so he could catch the first pitch. The Rays were playing the Mariners again, and again attendance was sparse, the upper deck a sea of blue. Evers settled in to watch, ignoring where the pitch was, focusing instead on the third row just to the left of the umpire. As if to answer his question with a cosmic Bronx cheer, Raymond, the team's mascot, a creature with blue fur not found anywhere in the natural world, flopped across the seats, shaking his fist behind Ichiro's back.

"You're going shack whacky," Evers said. "That's all."

The Mariners' ace, Felix Hernandez, was going for them, and King Felix was on. The game was fast. By the time Evers cracked his nightly beer, it was the sixth and the M's were up by a couple. It was then, just as King Felix caught Ben Zobrist looking, that Evers saw, three rows deep, in the same pinstriped suit he was buried in, his old business partner Leonard Wheeler.

Leonard Wheeler—always Leonard, never Lennie—was eating a hotdog and washing it down with what ESPN's *SportsCenter* smartasses were pleased to call "an adult beverage." For a moment, too startled for denial, Evers defaulted to the outrage the merest thought of Wheeler could call up from his gut even now. "You controlling son of a bitch!" he shouted, and dropped his own adult beverage, which he'd just been bringing to his lips. The can fell into the tray balanced on his lap and knocked it to the floor between his feet, where the chicken, instant mashed potatoes, and Birds Eye string beans (also of a color not found in the natural world) lay on the carpet in a foaming puddle of beer.

Evers didn't notice, only stared at his new television, which was so state-of-the-art that he sometimes felt he could simply hoick up a leg, duck his head to keep from bumping the frame, and step right into the picture. It was Wheeler, all right: same gold-rimmed glasses, same jutting jaw and weirdly plump lips, same head of flamboyant snow-white hair that made him look like a soap opera star—the mature lead who plays either a saintly doctor or a tycoon cuckolded by his sleazy trophy wife. There was no mistaking the oversized flag pin in his lapel either. He'd always worn that damned thing like a jackleg congressman. Ellie once joked that Lennie (when it was just them, they always called him that) probably tucked it under his pillow before he went to sleep.

Then the denial rushed in, swarming over his initial shock the way white blood cells swarm into a fresh cut. Evers closed his eyes, counted to five, then popped them wide, sure he'd see someone who just looked like Wheeler, or—perhaps worse—no one at all.

The shot had changed. Instead of a new batter stepping in, the camera focused on the Mariners' left fielder, who was doing a peculiar little dance.

"Never seen *that* one before," one of the Rays' announcers said. "What the heck is Wells up to, DeWayne?"

"Li'l crunk move, I 'spec," DeWayne Staats vamped, and they both chuckled.

Enough with the sparkling repartee, Evers thought. He shuffled his feet and managed to step on his beer-soaked chicken breast. *Go back to the damn home plate shot.*

As if the producer in his gadget-loaded broadcast truck had heard him, the shot switched back, but only for a second. Luke Scott hit a bullet to the Mariners' second baseman, and in the wink of an eye, the Trop was gone and Evers was left with the

Aflac duck, who was plugging holes in a rowboat even as it plugged insurance.

Evers got halfway up before his knees gave way and he collapsed back into his chair. The cushion made a tired wooshing sound. He took a deep breath, let it out, and felt a little stronger. This time he made it to his feet and trundled into the kitchen. He got the carpet cleaner from under the sink and read the instructions. Ellie wouldn't have needed to read them. Ellie would have simply made some half-irritated, half-amused comment ("You can dress him up, but you can't take him out" was a favorite) and gone to work making the mess disappear.

"That was not Lennie Wheeler," he told the empty living room as he came back. "No way it was."

The duck was gone, replaced by a man and his wife smooching on a patio. Soon they would go upstairs and make Viagra-aided love, because this was the age of knowing how to get things done. Evers, who also knew how to get things done (he'd read the instructions on the can, after all), fell on his knees, returned his sopping dinner to the tray in a series of plops, then sprayed a small cloud of Resolve on the remaining crud, knowing there'd probably be a stain anyway.

"Lennie Wheeler is as dead as Jacob Marley. I went to his funeral."

Indeed he had, and although his face had remained appropriately grave and regretful throughout, he'd enjoyed it.

Laughter might be the best medicine, but Dean Evers believed outliving your enemies was the best revenge.

Evers and Wheeler had met in business school, and had started Speedy Truck Rental on a shoestring after Wheeler had found what he called "a gaping hole the size of the Sumner Tunnel" in the New England market. In those early days Evers hadn't minded Wheeler's overbearing manner, perfectly summed up by a plaque on the man's office wall: WHEN I WANT MY OPINION, I'LL ASK YOU FOR IT. In those days, before Evers had begun to find his own way, he'd needed that kind of attitude. Wheeler, he sometimes thought, had been the steel in his spine. But young men grow up and develop their own ideas.

After twenty years Speedy had become the biggest independent truck rental outfit in New England, one of the few untainted by either organized crime or IRS problems. That was when Leonard Wheeler—never Lennie except when Evers and his wife were safely tucked into bed and giggling like a couple of kids—decided it was time to go national. Evers finally stood up on his hind legs and demurred. Not gently, as in previous disagreements, but firmly. Loudly, even. Everyone in the office had heard them, he had no doubt, even with the door closed.

The game came back on while he was waiting for the Resolve to set. Hellickson was still dealing for the Rays, and he was sharp. Not as sharp as Hernandez, though, and on any other night Evers would have been sending him brain-wave encouragement. Not tonight. Tonight he sat back on his heels at the base of his chair with his bony knees on either side of the stain he was trying to clean up, peering at the stands behind home plate.

There was Wheeler, still right there, now drinking a beer with one hand and holding a cell phone in the other. Just the sight of the phone filled Evers with outrage. Not because cell phones should be outlawed in ballparks like smoking, but because Wheeler had died of a heart attack long before such things were in general use. He had no *right* to it!

"Oh-oh, that's a *loo-oong* drive!" DeWayne Staats was bellowing. "Justin Smoak smoked *aaa-alll* of that one!"

The camera followed the ball into the nearly deserted stands, and lingered to watch two boys fighting over it. One emerged victorious and waved it at the camera, pumping his hips in a singularly obscene manner as he did so.

"Fuck you!" Evers shouted. "You're on TV, so what?"

He hardly ever used such language, but had he not said that very same thing to his partner during the argument over the expansion? Yes. Nor had it just been *Fuck you*. It had been *Fuck you, Lennie.*

"And what I did, you deserved it." He was dismayed to discover he was on the verge of tears. "You wouldn't take your foot off my neck, Leonard. I did what I had to do."

Now the camera returned to where it belonged, which was showing Smoak doing his home run trot, and pointing at the sky—well, *dome*—as he crossed home plate to the apathetic applause of the two dozen or so Mariner fans in attendance.

Kyle Seager stood in. Behind him, in the third row, the seat where Wheeler had been was empty.

It wasn't him, Evers thought, scrubbing the stain (that barbecue sauce was simply not going to come up). *It was just someone who looked like him.*

That hadn't worked very well with Young Doctor Young, and it didn't work at all now.

Evers turned off the TV and decided he'd go to bed early.

Useless. Sleep didn't come at ten or at midnight. At two o'clock he took one of Ellie's Ambien, hoping it wouldn't kill him—it was eighteen months past the expiration date. It didn't, but it didn't put him to sleep either. He took another half a tablet and lay in bed thinking of a plaque he'd kept in his own office. It said GIVE ME A LEVER LONG ENOUGH, A FULCRUM STRONG ENOUGH, AND I'LL MOVE THE WORLD. Far less arrogant than Wheeler's plaque, but perhaps more useful.

When Wheeler refused to let him out of the partnership agreement Evers had foolishly signed when he'd been young and humble, he'd needed that kind of lever to shift his partner. As it so happened, he had one. Leonard Wheeler had a taste for the occasional young boy. Oh, not *young* young, not jailbait, but college age. Wheeler's personal assistant, Martha, had confided to Evers one rum-soaked night at a convention in Denver that Wheeler was partial to the lifeguard type. Later, sober and remorseful, she'd begged him to never say a word to anyone. Wheeler was a good boss, she said, hard but good, and his wife was a dream. The same was true of his son and daughter.

Evers kept mum, even keeping this nugget from Ellie. If she'd known he intended to use any such scurrilous information to break the partnership agreement, she would have been horrified. *It's surely not necessary to stoop to that,* she would have said, and she would have believed it. El thought she understood the bind he was in, but she didn't. The most important thing she didn't understand was that it was *their* bind—hers and little Patrick's as well as his own. If Speedy went nationwide now, they'd be crushed by the giants within a year. Two at the outside. Evers was dead certain of it, and had the numbers to back it up. All they'd worked for would be washed away, and he had no intention of drowning in the sea of Lennie Wheeler's ambitions. It could not be allowed.

He hadn't opened with *Fuck you, Lennie.* First he tried the reasonable approach, using the latest spreadsheets to lay out his case. Their market share in New England was due to their ability to rent one-way and at hourly rates the big boys couldn't match. Because the area they covered was so compact, they could rebalance their entire inventory within three hours, where the big boys couldn't, and had to charge a premium. On September 1st, move-in day for the students,

Speedy owned Boston. Spread the fleet thin trying to cover the lower 48 and they'd have the same headaches as U-Haul and Penske—the same lumbering business model they purposely avoided and undersold. Why would they want to be like the other guys when they were killing the other guys? If Wheeler hadn't noticed, Penske was in Chapter 11, Thrifty too.

"Precisely," Wheeler said. "With the big boys on the sidelines, this is the perfect time. We *don't* try to be like them, Dean. We chop the country into regions and do what we already do."

"How does that work in the Northwest?" Evers asked. "Or the Southwest? Or even the Midwest? The country's too big."

"It may not be as profitable at first, but it won't take long. You've seen our competition. Eighteen months—two years tops—and we'll be absolutely killing them."

"We're already overextended, and now you want us to take on more debt."

As they went back and forth, Evers honestly believed in his argument. Even for a publicly owned company, the problems of capitalization and cash-flow were insurmountable—a judgment which would prove devastatingly true two decades later, when the downturn hit. But Lennie Wheeler was used to having his way, and nothing Evers said would dissuade him. Wheeler had already talked with several venture capital concerns and printed up a sleek-looking brochure. He planned to take his proposal directly to the shareholders, over Evers's protests, if necessary.

"I don't think you want to do that," Evers said.

"And why's that, Dean?"

He'd tried, really tried, to do this ethically, honorably. And he knew he was right; time would prove it. In business everything was a means to one end—survival. Evers felt it urgently then and still thought it true today: He had to save the company. Hence, the nuclear option.

"I don't think you want to do that because I don't think you'd like what I'd take to the shareholders' meeting. Or should I say, whom."

Wheeler laughed, a sick little chuckle. He stared at Evers as if he'd pulled a gun. "Whom?"

"We both know whom," Evers said.

Wheeler slowly rubbed a hand up the side of his face. "I was wondering why you walked in here like you'd already won something."

"We're not winning anything. We're avoiding a mistake that would lose us everything. I'm sorry it came to this. If you'd have just listened to me—"

"Fuck you, Dean," Wheeler said. "Don't try to apologize for blackmail. It's bad manners. And since it's just the two of us, why don't you roll those spreadsheets tight—that's the only way you'll get them up that narrow ass of yours—and admit the truth: you're a coward. Always were."

Within a year, Evers bought him out. The split was expensive, and, in retrospect, a better deal than Wheeler deserved.

Lennie left New England, then his wife, and finally, in an ER in Palm Springs, this earthly vale of tears. Out of respect, Evers flew west for the funeral, at which, not surprisingly, there were no lifeguard types, and, of the family, only the daughter, who dryly thanked Evers for coming. He didn't say the first thought which had come into his mind: *Sarcasm doesn't become fat girls, dear.* A few years later, after a thorough vetting of the numbers and fueled by Bain Capital, Speedy actually did go national, using a streamlined version of their old regional plan. That Evers had been right—that it ended with Speedy's lawyers filing the same Chapter 11 briefs as their vanquished rivals—was little vindication. He came out of it with a goodly sum, however, and that was.

The funny thing was that with a minimum of digging—an offhand question or three to Martha, a keen read of her blinking—Wheeler could have bought himself an ironclad insurance policy. When Evers realized this, he gently dropped her, which, because they both had a conscience, was actually a relief. Their fling had run its more than pleasant course, and rather than fire her, he kept her closer, making her his executive assistant at double the salary, working beside her day-in day-out until, eventually, she accepted a lavish early retirement package. At her farewell party, he made a speech and gave her a Honda Goldwing and a peck on the cheek, to raised glasses and warm applause. The affair ended with a slideshow featuring Martha on her old Harley Tri-Glide, while George Thorogood sang "Ride On, Josephine."

It was a rare moment for Evers, a happy parting. Beyond the silly intrigue, he'd always liked Martha, her brash laugh and the way she hummed to herself as she typed, a pencil tucked behind one ear. What he said in his speech—that she wasn't merely an assistant but a dear and trusted friend—was true. Though he hadn't spoken to her in ages, of all the people he'd worked with, she was the only one he missed. Drowsing now as the Ambien kicked in, he wondered hazily if she was still alive, or if, tomorrow, he'd turn on the game and find her behind home, wearing the sleeveless yellow sundress with the daisies he liked.

He rose at eight—a full hour past his usual time—and stooped to pick the paper from the mat. He checked the sports page and discovered the Rays had the night off. That was all right; there was always *CSI.* Evers showered, ate a healthy breakfast in which wheat germ played a major role, then sat down to track Young Doctor Young on the computer. When that marvel of the 21st century failed (or maybe he just wasn't doing it right; Ellie had always been the computer whiz), he picked up the telephone. According to the morgue desk at the Shrewsbury *Herald-Crier*, the dental bogeyman of Evers's childhood had died in 1978. Amazingly, he'd been only 59, nearly a decade younger than Evers was now. Evers pondered the unknowable: Was his life cut short by the war, Luckies, dentistry, or all three?

There was nothing remarkable in his obituary, just the usual survived by and funeral home info. Evers had had absolutely nothing to do with the drunk old butcher's demise, just the bad luck to be his victim. Exonerated, that night he raised an extra glass or four to Dr. Young. He ordered in, but it took forever, arriving after he was well in the bag. *CSI* turned out to be one he'd seen before, and all the sitcoms were stupid. Where was Bob Newhart when you needed him? Evers brushed his teeth, took two of Ellie's Ambien, then stood swaying in front of the bathroom mirror, his eyes bleeding. "Give me a liver long enough," he said, "and I'll move the fucking world."

He slept late again, recovering with instant coffee and oatmeal, and was pleased to see in the paper that the Sox were coming in for a big weekend series. He celebrated the opener with steak, setting the DVR to capture whatever malevolent spirit his past might vomit up. If it happened, this time he'd be ready.

It did, in the seventh inning of a tie game, on a key play at the plate. He would have missed it if he'd gone off to do the dishes, but by then he was poised on the edge of the sofa, totally into the contest and concentrating on every pitch. Longoria doubled to the gap in left-center, and Upton tried to score from first. The throw beat him but was wide, up the first base line. As Sox catcher Kelly Shoppach lunged toward home with a sweep tag, directly behind the screen a scrawny, freckle-faced boy not more than nine rose from his seat.

A FACE IN THE CROWD

His haircut was what used to be called a dutchboy, or, if you were taunting this particular fellow at school, a soup-bowl. "Hey, Soup!" they used to hound him in gym, pummeling him, turning every game into Smear the Queer. "Hey, Soupy, Soup, Soupy!"

His name was Lester Embree, and here in the shadowy Trop he wore the same threadbare red-and-blue striped shirt and bleached, patched-at-the-knees Tuffskins he always seemed to have on that spring of 1954. He was white but he lived in the black part of town behind the fairgrounds. He had no father, and the kindest rumor about his mother said she worked in the laundry at St. Joe's hospital. In the middle of the school year he'd come to Shrewsbury from some hick town in Tennessee, a move that seemed foolish, a dunderheaded affront to Evers and his cadre of buddies. They delighted in imitating his soft drawl, drawing out the halting answers he gave in class into Foghorn Leghorn monologues. "I say, I say, Miss Pritchett, ma'am, I do declayuh I have done done dooty in these heah britches."

On screen, Upton leapt to his feet, looking back at the sprawled catcher and signaling safe just as the umpire punched the air with a clenched fist. A different camera zoomed out to show Joe Maddon charging from the dugout in high dudgeon. The sellout crowd was going wild.

In the replay—even before Evers paused and ran it back with the clicker—Lester Embree and his doofy bowl cut were visible above the FOX 13 ad recessed into the wall's blue padding, and then, as Upton clearly evaded the tag with a nifty hook slide, the quiet boy Evers and his friends had witnessed being pulled wrinkled and fingerless from Marsden's Pond rose and pointed one fish-nibbled stub not at the play developing right in front of him, but, as if he could see into the air-conditioned, dimly lit condo, directly at Evers. His lips were moving, and it didn't look like he was saying *kill the ump.*

"Come on," Evers scoffed, as if at the bad call. "Jesus, I was a *kid.*"

The TV returned to live action—very lively, in fact. Joe Maddon and the home plate ump stood toe to toe and nose to nose. Both were jawing away, and you didn't have to be a fortune-teller to know that Maddon would soon be following the game from the clubhouse. Evers had no interest in watching the Rays' manager get the hook. He used his remote to run the picture back to where Lester Embree had come into view.

Maybe he won't be there, Evers thought. *Maybe you can't DVR ghosts any more than you can see vampires in a mirror.*

Only Lester Embree was right there in the stands—in the expensive seats, no less—and Evers suddenly remembered the day at Fairlawn Grammar when old Soupy had been waiting at Evers's locker. Just seeing him there had made Evers want to haul off and paste him one. The little fucker was trespassing, after all. *They'll stop if you tell 'em to,* Soupy had said in that crackerbarrel drawl of his. *Even Kaz will stop.*

He'd been talking about Chuckie Kazmierski, only no one called him Chuckie, not even now. Evers could attest to that, because Kaz was the only friend from his childhood who was still a friend. He lived in Punta Gorda, and sometimes they got together for a round of golf. Just two happy retirees, one divorced, one a widower. They reminisced a lot—really, what else were old men good for?—but it had been years since they talked about Soupy Embree. Evers had to wonder now just why that was. Shame? Guilt? Maybe on his part, but probably not on Kaz's. As the youngest of six brothers and the runt of their scruffy pack, Kaz had had to fight for every inch of respect. He'd earned his spot as top dog the hard way, with knuckles and blood, and he took Lester Embree's helplessness as a personal insult. No one had ever given him a break, and now this whingeing hillbilly was asking for a free pass? "Nothing's free," Kaz used to say, shaking his head as if it was a sad truth. "Somehow, some way, somebody got to pay."

Probably Kaz doesn't even remember, Evers thought. *Neither did I, till tonight.* Tonight he was having total recall. Mostly what he remembered was the kid's pleading eyes that day by his locker. Big and blue and soft. And that wheedling, cornpone voice, begging him, like it was really in his power to do it.

You're the one Kaz and the rest of them listen to. Gimme a break, won't you? Ah'll give you money. Two bucks a week, that's mah whole allowance. All Ah want's to get along?

Little as he liked to, Evers could remember his answer, delivered in a jeering mockery of the boy's accent: *If'n all you want's to git along, you git along raht out of heah, Soupy. Ah don't want yoah money, hit's prob'ly crawlin was fag germs.*

A loyal lieutenant (not the general, as Lester Embree had assumed), Evers immediately brought the matter to Kaz, embellishing the scene further, laughing at his own drawl. Later, in the shadow of the flagpole, he egged on Kaz from the nervous circle surrounding the fight. Technically, it wasn't a fight at all, because Soupy never defended himself. He folded at Kaz's first blow, curling into a ball on the ground while Kaz slugged and kicked him at will. And then, as if he'd tired, Kaz straddled him, grabbed his wrists and pinned his arms back above his head. Soupy was weeping, his split lip blowing bloody bubbles. In the tussle, his red-and-blue striped shirt had ripped, the fishbelly skin of his chest showing through a fist-sized hole. He didn't resist as Kaz let go of his wrists, took hold of the tear in his shirt with both hands and ripped it apart. The collar wouldn't give, and Kaz tugged it off over Soupy's ears in three hard jerks, then stood and twirled the shreds over his head like a lasso before flinging it down on Soupy and walking away. What astonished Evers, besides the inner wildness Kaz had tapped and the style with which he'd destroyed his opponent, was how fast it all happened. In total, it had taken maybe two minutes. The teachers still hadn't even made it outside.

When the kid disappeared a week later, Evers and his pals thought he must have run away. Soupy's mother thought differently. He liked to go on wildlife walks, she said. He was a dreamy boy, he might have gotten lost. There was a massive search of the nearby woods, including baying teams of bloodhounds brought from Boston. As Boy Scouts, Evers and his friends were in on it. They heard the commotion at the dam end of Marsden's Pond and came running. Later, when they saw the eyeless thing that rose dripping from the spillway, they would all wish they hadn't.

And now, thanks to God only knew what agency, here was Lester Embree at Tropicana Field, standing with the other fans watching the play at the plate. His fingers were mostly gone, but he still seemed to have his thumbs. His eyes and nose, too. Well, most of his nose. Lester was looking through the television screen at Dean Evers, just like Miss Nancy looking through her magic mirror on the old *Romper Room* show. "Romper-stomper-bomper-boo," Miss Nancy liked to chant in the way-back-when. "My magic mirror can see you."

Lester's pointing finger-stub. Lester's moving mouth. Saying what? Evers only had to watch it twice to be sure: *You murdered me.*

"Not true!" he yelled at the boy in the red-and-blue striped shirt. "Not true! *You fell in Marsden's! You fell in the pond! You fell in the pond and it was your own goddamned fault!*"

He turned off the TV and went to bed. He lay there awhile thrumming like a wire, then got up and took two Ambien, washing them down with a healthy knock of scotch. The pill-and-booze combo killed the thrumming, at least, but he still lay wakeful, staring into the dark with eyes that felt as large and smooth as brass doorknobs. At three he turned the clock-radio around to face the wall. At five, as the first traces of dawn back-lit the drapes, a comforting thought came to him. He wished he could share this comforting thought with Soupy Embree, but since he couldn't, he did the next best thing and spoke it aloud.

"If it were possible to go back in a time machine and change the stupid things some of us did in grammar school and junior high, Soups old buddy, that gadget would be booked up right into the twenty-third century."

Exactamundo. You couldn't blame kids. Grownups knew better, but kids were stupid by nature. Sometimes malevolent by nature too. He seemed to remember something about a girl in New Zealand who'd bludgeoned her best friend's mother to death with a brick. She'd hit the poor woman fifty times or more with that old brick, and when the girl was found guilty she went to jail for...what? Seven years? Five? Less? When she got out, she went to England and became an airline stewardess. Later she became a very popular mystery novelist. Who'd told him that story? Ellie, of course. El had been a great reader of mysteries, always trying—and often succeeding—in guessing whodunit.

"Soupy," he told his lightening bedroom, "you can't blame me. I plead diminished capacity." That actually made him smile.

As if it had just been waiting for this conclusion, another comforting thought arose. *I don't need to watch the game tonight. Nothing's forcing me to.*

That was finally enough to send him off. He woke shortly after noon, the first time he'd slept so late since college. In the kitchen he briefly considered the oatmeal, then fried himself three eggs in butter. He would have tossed in some bacon, if he'd had any. He did the next-best thing, adding it to the grocery list stuck to the fridge with a cucumber magnet.

"No game tonight for me," he told the empty condo. "Ah b'leeve Ah maht..."

He heard what his voice was doing and stopped, bewildered. It came to him that he might not be suffering from dementia or early-onset Alzheimer's; he might be having your ordinary everyday garden-variety nervous breakdown. That seemed a perfectly reasonable explanation for recent events, but knowledge was power. If you saw what was happening, you could stop it, right?

"I believe I might go out to a movie," he said in his own voice. Quietly. Reasonably. "That's all I meant to say."

In the end, he decided against a film. Although there were twenty screens in the immediate area, he could find nothing he wanted to watch on a single one of them. He went to the Publix instead, where he picked up a basketful of goodies (including a pound of the good thick-sliced pepper bacon Ellie loved). He started for the ten-items-or-less checkout lane, saw the girl at the register was wearing a Rays shirt with Matt Joyce's number 20 on the back, and diverted to one of the other lanes instead. That took longer, but he told himself he didn't mind. He also told himself he wasn't thinking about how someone would be singing the National Anthem at the Trop right now. He'd picked up the new Harlan Coben in paperback, a little literary bacon to go with the literal variety. He'd read it tonight. Baseball couldn't match up to Coben's patented terror-in-the-burbs, not even when it was Jon Lester matched up against Matt Moore. How had he ever become interested in such a slow, boring sport to begin with?

He put away his groceries and settled onto the sofa. The Coben was terrific, and he got into it right away. Evers was so immersed that he didn't realize he'd picked up the TV remote, but when he got to the end of chapter six and decided to break for a small piece of Pepperidge Farm lemon cake, the gadget was right there in his hand.

Won't hurt to check the score, he thought. *Just a quick peek, and off it goes.*

The Rays were up one to nothing in the eighth, and DeWayne Staats was so excited he was burbling. "Don't want to talk about what's going on with Matt Moore tonight, folks—I'm old-school—but let's just say that the bases have been devoid of Crimson Hose."

No-hitter, Evers thought. *Moore's pitching a damn no-hitter and I've been missing it.*

Close-up on Moore. He was sweating, even in the Trop's constant 72 degrees. He went into his motion, the picture changed to the home plate shot, and there in the third row was Dean Evers's dead wife, wearing the same tennis whites she'd had on the day of her first stroke. He would have recognized that blue piping anywhere.

Ellie was deeply tan, as she always was by this time of summer, and as was the case more often than not at the ballpark, she was ignoring the game entirely, poking at her iPhone instead. For an unfocused moment, Evers wondered who she was texting—someone here, or someone in the afterlife?—when, in his pocket, his cellphone buzzed.

She raised the phone to her ear and gave him a little wave.

Pick up, she mouthed, and pointed to her phone.

Evers shook his head no slowly.

His phone vibrated again, like a mild shock applied to his thigh.

"No," he said to the TV, and thought, logically: She can just leave a message.

Ellie shook her phone at him.

"This is wrong," he said. Because Ellie wasn't like Soupy Embree or Lennie Wheeler or Young Dr. Young. She loved him—of that Evers was sure—and he loved her. Forty-six years meant something, especially nowadays.

He searched her face. She seemed to be smiling, and while he didn't have a speech prepared, he guessed he did want to tell her how much he missed her, and what his days were like, and how he wished he was closer to Pat and Sue and the grandkids, because, really, there was no one else he could talk to.

He dug the phone from his pocket. Though he'd deactivated her account months ago, the number that came up was hers.

On TV, Moore was pacing behind the mound, juggling the rosin bag on the back of his pitching hand.

And then there she was, right behind David Ortiz, holding up her phone.

He pressed TALK.

"Hello?" he said.

"Finally," she said. "Why didn't you pick up?"

"I don't know. It's kind of weird, don't you think?"

"What's weird?"

"I don't know. You not being here and all."

"Dead, you mean. Me being dead."

"That."

"So you don't want to talk to me because I'm dead."

"No," he said. "I always want to talk to you." He smiled—at least, he thought he was smiling. He'd have to check the mirror to be sure, because his face felt frozen. "You're wanted, sweetheart, dead or alive."

"You're such a liar. That's one thing I always hated about you. And fucking Martha, of course. I wasn't a big fan of that either."

What could he say to that? Nothing. So he sat silent.

"Did you think I didn't know?" she said. "That's another thing I hated about you, thinking I didn't know what was going on. It was so obvious. A couple of times you came home still stinking of her perfume. Juicy Couture. Not the most subtle of scents. But then, you were never the most subtle guy, Dean."

"I miss you, El."

"Okay, yes, I miss you too. That's not the point."

"I love you."

"Stop trying to press my buttons, all right? I need to do this. I didn't say anything before because I needed to keep everything together and make everything work. That's who I am. Or was, anyway. And I did. But you hurt me. You *cut* me."

"I'm sorr—"

"Please, Dean. I only have a couple minutes left, so for once in your life shut up and listen. You hurt me, and it wasn't just with Martha. And although I'm pretty sure Martha was the only one you slept with—"

That stung. "Of course she wa—"

"—don't expect any Brownie points for that. You didn't have time to cheat on me with anyone outside the company because you were always there. Even when you were here you were there. I understood that, and maybe that was my fault for not sticking up for myself, but the one it really wasn't fair to was Patrick. You wonder why you never see him, it's because you were never there for him. You were always off in Denver or Seattle at some sales meeting or something. Selfishness is learned behavior, you know."

This criticism Evers had heard many times before, in many forms, and his attention waned. Moore had gone 3-2 on Papi. *Devoid*, Staats had said. Was Matt Moore really throwing a perfect game?

"You were always too worried about what you were doing, and not enough about the rest of us. You thought bringing home the bacon was enough."

I did, he almost told her. *I did bring home the bacon. Just tonight.*

"Dean? Are you hearing me? Do you understand what I'm telling you?"

"Yes," Evers said, just as the pitch from Moore caught the outside corner and the ump rang up Ortiz. "*Yes!*"

"I know that yes! God damn you, are you watching the stupid game?"

"Of course I'm watching the game." Though now it was a truck commercial. A grinning man—one who undoubtedly knew how to get things done—was driving through mud at a suicidal speed.

"I don't know why I called. You're hopeless."

"I'm not," Evers said. "I miss you."

"Jesus, why do I even bother? Forget it. Goodbye."

"Don't!" he said.

"I tried to be nice—that's the story of my life. I tried to be nice and look where it got me. People like you *eat* nice. Goodbye, Dean."

"I love you," he repeated, but she was gone, and when the game came back on, the woman with the sparkly top was in Ellie's seat. The woman with the sparkly top was a Tropicana Field regular. Sometimes the top was blue and sometimes it was green, but it was always sparkly. Probably so the folks at home could pick her out. As if she'd caught the thought, she waved. Evers waved back. "Yeah, bitch, I see you. You're on TV, bitch, good fucking job."

He got up and poured himself a scotch.

In the ninth Ellsbury snuck a seeing-eye single through the right side, and the crowd rose and applauded Moore for his effort. Evers turned the game off and sat before the dark screen, mulling what Ellie had said.

Unlike Soupy Embree's accusation, Ellie's was true. *Mostly true*, he amended, then changed it to *at least partly true.* She knew him better than anyone in the world—this world or any other—but she'd never been willing to give him the credit he deserved. He was, after all, the one who'd put groceries in the refrigerator all those years, some pretty high grade bacon. He was also the one who'd *paid* for the refrigerator—a top-of-the-line Sub-Zero, thank you very much. He'd paid for her Audi. And her tennis club dues. And her massage therapist. And all the stuff she bought from the catalogues. And hey, let's not forget Patrick's college tuition! Evers had had to put together a jackleg combination of scholarships, loan packages, and shit summer jobs to get through school, but Patrick had gotten a full boat from his old man. The old man he was too busy to call these days.

She comes back from the dead, and why? To complain. And to do it on the goddam iPhone I paid for.

He thought of an old saying and wished he'd quoted it to Ellie while he still had the chance: "Money can't buy happiness, but it allows one to endure unhappiness in relative comfort."

That might have shut her up.

The more he considered their life together—and there was nothing like talking to your dead spouse while you looked at her in a club seat to make you consider such things—the more he thought that while he hadn't been perfect, he'd still been all right. He did love her and Patrick, and had always tried to be kind to them. He'd worked hard to give them everything he never had, thinking he was doing the right thing. If it wasn't enough, there was nothing he could do about it now. As for the thing with Martha...some kinds of fucking were meaningless. Men understood that—*Kaz* certainly would have understood it—but women did not.

In bed, dropping into a blissful oblivion that was three parts Ambien and two parts scotch, it came to him that Ellie's rant was strangely freeing. Who else could they (whoever *they* were) send to bedevil him? Who could make him feel any worse? His mother? His father? He'd loved them, but not as he'd loved Ellie. Miss Pritchett? His Uncle Elmer who used to tickle him till he wet his pants?

Snuggling deeper into the covers, Evers actually snickered at that. No, the worst had happened. And although there would be another great match-up tomorrow night at the Trop—Josh Beckett squaring off against James Shields—he didn't have to watch. His last thought was that from now on, he'd have more time to read. Lee Child, maybe. He'd been meaning to get to those Lee Child books.

But first he had the Harlan Coben to finish. He spent the afternoon lost in the green, pitiless suburbs. As the sun went down on another St. Petersburg Sunday, he was into the last fifty pages or so, and racing along. That was when his phone buzzed. He picked it up gingerly—the way a man might pick up a loaded mousetrap—and looked at the readout. What he saw there was a relief. The call was from Kaz, and unless his old pal had suffered a fatal heart attack (not entirely out of the question; he was a good thirty pounds overweight), he was calling from Punta Gorda rather than the afterlife.

Still, Evers was cautious; given recent events, he had every reason to be. "Kaz, is that you?"

"Who the hell else would it be?" Kaz boomed. Evers winced and held the phone away from his ear. "Barack fucking Obama?"

Evers laughed feebly. "No, I just—"

"Fuckin' Dino Martino! You suck, buddy! Front row seats, and you didn't even call me?"

From far away, Evers heard himself say: "I only had one ticket." He looked at his watch. Twenty past eight. It should have been the second inning by now—unless the Rays and Red Sox were the eight o'clock Sunday night game on ESPN.

He reached for the remote.

Kaz, meanwhile, was laughing. The way he'd laughed that day in the schoolyard. It had been higher-pitched then, but otherwise it was just the same. *He* was just the same. It was a depressing thought. "Yeah, yeah, I'm just yankin' your ball-sack. How's the view from there?"

"Great," Evers said, pushing the power button on the remote. Fox 13 was showing some old movie with Bruce Willis blowing things up. He punched 29 and ESPN came on. Shields was dealing to Dustin Pedroia, second in the Sox lineup. The game had just started.

I'm doomed to baseball, Evers thought.

"Dino? Earth to Dino Martino! You still there?"

"I'm here," he said, and turned up the volume. Pedroia flailed and missed. The crowd roared; those irritating cowbells the Rays fans favored clanged with maniacal fervor. "Pedie just struck out."

"No shit, I ain't blind, Stevie Wonder. The Rays Rooters are pumped up, huh?"

"Totally pumped," Evers said hollowly. "Great night for a ballgame."

Now Adrian Gonzalez was stepping in. And there, sitting in the first row right behind the screen, doing a fair impersonation of a craggy old snowbird playing out his golden years in the Sunshine State, was Dean Patrick Evers.

He was wearing a ridiculous foam finger, and although he couldn't read it, not even in HD, he knew what it said: RAYS ARE #1. Evers at home stared at Evers behind home with the phone against his ear. Evers at the park stared back, holding the selfsame phone in the hand that wasn't wearing the foam finger. With a sense of outrage that not even his stunned amazement could completely smother, he saw that Ballpark Evers was wearing a Rays jersey. *Never*, he thought. *Those are traitor colors.*

"There you are!" Kaz shouted exultantly. "Shake me a wave, buddy!"

Evers at the ballpark raised the foam finger and waved it solemnly, like an oversized windshield wiper. Evers at home, on autopilot, did the same with his free hand.

"Love the shirt, Dino," Kaz said. "Seeing you in Rays colors is like seeing Doris Day topless." He snickered.

"I had to wear it," Evers said. "The guy who gave me the ticket insisted. Listen, I've gotta go. Want to grab a beer and a d—ohmygod, there it goes!"

Gonzo had launched a long drive, high and deep.

"Drink one for me!" Kaz shouted.

On Evers's expensive TV, Gonzalez was lumbering around the bases. As he watched, Evers suddenly understood what he had to do. There was only one way to put an end to this cosmic joke. On a Sunday night, downtown St. Pete would be deserted. If he took a taxi, he could be at the Trop by the end of the second inning. Maybe even sooner.

"Kaz?"

"Yeah, buddy?"

"We should either have been nicer to Lester Embree, or left him alone."

He pushed END before Kaz could reply. He turned off the TV. Then he went into his bedroom, rooted through the folded shirts in his bureau, and found his beloved Curt Schilling jersey, the one with the bloody sock on the front and WHY NOT US? on the back. Schilling had been The Man, afraid of nothing. When the Evers in the Rays shirt saw him in this one, he'd fade away like the bad dream he was and all of this would end.

Evers yanked the shirt on and called a cab. There was one nearby that had just dropped off a fare, and the streets were as deserted as Evers had expected. The cabbie had the game on the radio. The Sox were still batting in the top half of the second when he pulled up to the main gate.

"You'll have to settle for nosebleeds," the cabbie said. "Sox-Rays, that's a hot ticket."

"I've got one right behind home plate," Evers said. "Stop somewhere they've got the game on, you might see me. Look for the shirt with the bloody sock on it."

"I heard that fuckin' hoser's video game business went broke," the cabbie said as Evers handed him a ten. He looked, saw Evers still sitting in the back seat with the door open, and reluctantly made change. From it, Evers handed him a single rumpled simoleon.

"Guy with a front row seat should be able to do better'n that for a tip," the cabbie grumbled.

"Guy with half a brain in his head should keep his mouth shut about the Big Schill," Evers said. "If he wants a better tip, that is." He slipped out, slammed the door and headed for the entrance.

"*Fuck you, Boston!*" the cabbie shouted.

Without turning around, Evers hoisted a middle finger—real, not foam.

The concourse was all but empty, the sound of the crowd inside the stadium a hollow surf-boom. It was a sellout, the LED signs above the shuttered ticket windows bragged. There was only one window still open, all the way down at the end, the WILL CALL.

Yes, Evers thought, because they *will* call, won't they? He headed for it like a man on rails.

"Help you, sir?" the pretty ticket-agent asked, and was that Juicy Couture she was wearing? Surely not. He remembered

Martha saying, *It's my slut perfume. I only wear it for you.* She'd been willing to do things Ellie wouldn't dream of, things he remembered at all the wrong times.

"*Help* you, sir?"

"Sorry," Evers said. "Had a little senior moment there."

She smiled dutifully.

"Do you happen to have a ticket for Evers? Dean Evers?"

There was no hesitation, no thumbing through a whole box of envelopes, because there was only one left. It had his name on it. She slid it through the gap in the glass. "Enjoy the game."

"We'll see," Evers said.

He made for Gate A, opening the envelope and taking out the ticket. A piece of paper was clipped to it, just four words below the Rays logo: **COMPLIMENTS OF THE MANAGEMENT**. He strode briskly up the ramp and handed the ticket to a crusty usher who was standing there and watching as Elliot Johnson dug in against Josh Beckett. At the very least, the geezer was a good half century older than his employers. Like so many of his kind, he was in no hurry. It was one reason Evers no longer drove.

"Nice seat," the usher said, raising his eyebrows. "Just about the best in the house. And you show up late." He gave a disapproving headshake.

"I would have been here sooner," Evers said, "but my wife died."

The usher froze in the act of turning away, Evers's ticket in hand.

"Gotcha," Evers said, smiling and pointing a playful finger-gun. "That one never fails."

The usher didn't look amused. "Follow me, sir."

Down and down the steep steps they went. The usher was in worse shape than Evers, all wattle and liver spots, and by the time they reached the front row, Johnson was headed back to the dugout, a strikeout victim. Evers's seat was the only empty one—or not quite empty. Leaning against the back was a large blue foam finger that blasphemed: RAYS ARE #1.

My seat, Evers thought, and as he picked the offending finger up and sat down he saw, with only the slightest surprise, that he was no longer wearing his treasured Schilling jersey. Somewhere between the cab and this ridiculous, padded Captain Kirk perch, it had been replaced by a turquoise Rays shirt. And although he couldn't see the back, he knew what it said: MATT YOUNG 20.

"Young Matt Young," he said, a crack that his neighbors—neither of whom he recognized—pointedly ignored. He craned around, searching the section for Ellie and Soupy Embree and Lennie Wheeler, but it was just a mix of anonymous Rays and Sox fans. He didn't even see the sparkly top lady.

Between pitches, as he was twisted around trying to see behind him, the guy on his right tapped Evers's arm and pointed to the Jumbotron just in time for him to catch a grotesquely magnified version of himself turning around.

"You missed yourself," the guy said.

"That's all right," Evers said. "I've been on TV enough lately."

Before Beckett could decide between his fastball and his slider, Evers's phone buzzed in his pocket.

Can't even watch the game in peace.

"Yello," he said.

"Who'm I talkin' to?" The voice of Chuckie Kazmierski was high and truculent, his I'm-ready-to-fight voice. Evers knew it well, had heard it often over the long arc of years stretching between Fairlawn Grammar and this seat at Tropicana Field, where the light was always dingy and the stars were never seen. "That you, Dino?"

"Who else? Bruce Willis?" Beckett missed low and away. The crowd rang their idiotic cowbells.

"Dino Martino, right?"

Jesus, Evers thought, *next he'll be saying who's on first and I'll be saying what's on second.*

"Yes, Kaz, the artist also known as Dean Patrick Evers. We ate paste together in the second grade, remember? Probably too much."

"It *is* you!" Kaz shouted, making Evers jerk the phone away from his ear. "I *told* that cop he was full of shit! Detective Kelly, my ass."

"What in hell are you talking about?"

"Some ass-knot pretending to be a cop's what I'm talkin' about. I knew it couldn't be real, he sounded too fuckin' official."

"Huh," Evers said. "An official official, imagine that."

"Guy tells me you're dead, so I go, if he's dead, how come I just talked to him on the phone? And the cop—the *so-called* cop—he goes, I think you're mistaken, sir. You must have talked to someone else. And *I* go, how come I just now saw him on TV at the Rays game? And this so-called cop goes, either you saw someone who looked like him or someone who looks like him is dead in his apartment. You believe this shit?"

Beckett bounced one off the plate. He was all over the place. The crowd was loving it. "If it wasn't a prank, I guess someone made a big mistake."

"Ya *think*?" Kaz gave his trademark laugh, low and raspy. "Especially since I'm talkin' to you right fuckin' now."

"You called to make sure I was still alive, huh?"

"Yeah." Now that he was settling down, Kaz seemed puzzled by this.

"Tell me something—if I'd turned out to be dead after all, would you have left a voicemail?"

"What? Jesus, I don't know." Kaz seemed more puzzled than ever, but that was nothing new. He'd always been puzzled. By events, by other people, probably by his own beating heart. Evers supposed that was part of why he'd so often been angry. Even when he wasn't angry, he was *ready* to be angry.

I'm speaking of him in the past tense, Evers realized.

"The guy I talked to said they found you at your place. Said you'd been dead for a while too."

The guy next to Evers nudged him again. "Lookin' good, buddy," he said.

On the Jumbotron, shocking in its homely familiarity, was Evers's darkened bedroom. In the middle of the bed he'd shared with Ellie, the pillowtop king that was now too big for him, Evers lay still and pale, his eyes half-lidded, his lips purplish, his mouth a stiff rictus. Foam had dried like old spider webs on his chin.

When Evers turned to his seatmate, wanting to confirm what he was seeing, the seat beside him—the row, the section, the whole Tropicana Dome—was empty. And yet the players kept playing.

"They said you killed yourself."

"I didn't kill myself," Evers replied, and thought: *That damn expired Ambien. And maybe putting it with the scotch wasn't such a great idea. How long has it been? Since Friday night?*

"I know, it didn't sound like you."

"So, are you watching the game?"

"I turned it off. Fuckin' cop—that fuckin' ass-knot—upset me."

"Turn it on again," Evers said.

"Okay," Kaz said. "Lemme grab the remote."

"You know, we should have been nicer to Lester Embree."

"Water over the dam, old buddy. Or under the bridge. Or whatever the fuck it is."

"Maybe not. From now on, don't be so angry. Try to be nicer to people. Try to be nicer to everyone. Do that for me, will you, Kaz?"

"What the Christ is wrong with you? You sound like a fuckin' Hallmark card on Mother's Day."

"I suppose I do," Evers said. He found this a very sad idea, somehow. On the mound, Beckett was peering in for the sign.

"Hey, Dino! There you are! You sure don't *look* dead." Kaz gave out his old rusty cackle.

"I don't feel it."

"I was scared there for a minute," Kaz said. "Fuckin' crank yanker. Wonder how he got my number."

"Dunno," Evers said, surveying the empty park. Though of course he knew. After Ellie died, of the nine million people in Tampa-St. Pete, Kaz was the only person he could put down as an emergency contact. And that idea was sadder still.

"All right, buddy, I'll let you get back to the game. Maybe golf next week if it doesn't rain."

"We'll see," Evers said. "Stay cool, Kazzie, and—"

Kaz joined him then, and they chanted the last line together, as they had many, many times before: "*Don't let the bastards get you down!*"

That was it, it was over. He sensed things moving again, a flurry behind him, at the periphery of his vision. He looked around, phone in hand, and saw the spotted usher creakily leading his Uncle Elmer and Aunt June and several girls he'd dated in high school down the stairs, including the one who'd been sort of semiconscious—or maybe *unconscious* would be closer to the truth—when he'd had her. Behind them came Miss Pritchett with her hair down for once, and Mrs. Carlisle from the drugstore, and the Jansens, the elderly neighbors whose deposit bottles he'd stolen off their backporch. From the other side, as if it were a company outing, a second, equally ancient usher was filling in the rows at the top of the section with former Speedy employees, a number of them in their blue uniforms. He recognized Don Blanton, who'd been questioned during a child pornography investigation in the mid-nineties and had hung himself in his Malden garage. Evers remembered how shocked he'd been, both by the idea of someone he knew possibly being involved in kiddie-porn and by Don's final action. He'd always liked the man, and hadn't wanted to let him go, but with that kind of accusation hanging over his head, what else could he do? The reputation of a company's employees was part of its bottom line.

He still had some battery left. What the hell, he thought. It was a big game. They were probably watching on the Cape.

"Hey, Dad," Pat answered.

"You watching the game?"

"The kids are. The grownups are playing cards."

Next to the first usher stood Lennie Wheeler's daughter, still in her black crepe and veil. She pointed like a dark spectre at Evers. She'd lost all her baby fat, and Evers wondered if that had happened before she died, or after.

"Go look at the game, son."

"Hang on," Pat said, followed by the screek of a chair. "Okay, I'm watching."

"Right behind home,in the front row."

"What am I looking at?"

Evers stood up behind the netting and waved his blue foam finger. "Do you see me?"

"No, where are you?"

Young Dr. Young hobbled down the steep stairs on his bad leg, using the seat backs to steady himself. On his smock, like a medal, was a coffee-colored splotch of dried blood.

"Do you see me now?" Evers took the phone from his ear and waved both arms over his head as if he was flagging a train. The grotesque finger nodded back and forth.

"No."

So, no.

Which was fine. Which was actually better.

"Be good, Patty," Evers said. "I love you."

He hit END CALL as, all around the park, the sections were filling in. He couldn't see who'd come to spend eternity with him in peanut heaven or the far reaches of the outfield, but the premium seats were going fast. Here came the ushers with the shambling, rag-clad remnants of Soupy Embree, and then his mother, haggard after a double shift, and Lennie Wheeler in his pinstriped funeral suit and his Grandfather Lincoln with his cane and Martha and Ellie and his mother and father and all the people he'd ever wronged in his life. As they filed into his row from both sides, he stuck his phone in his pocket and took his seat again, pulling off the foam finger as he did. He propped it on the now unoccupied seat to his left. Saving it for Kaz. Because he was sure Kaz would be joining them at some point, after seeing him on TV, and calling him. If Evers had learned anything about how this worked, it was that the two of them weren't done talking just yet.

A cheer erupted, and the rattle of cowbells. The Rays were still hitting. Down the right field line, though it was far too early, some loudmouth was exhorting the crowd to start the wave. As always when distracted from the action, Evers checked the scoreboard to catch up. It was only the third and Beckett had already thrown sixty pitches. The way things were looking, it was going to be a long game.